THE NEAR ENOUGH

Stories

MICHAEL C. KEITH

copyright © 2015 by Michael Keith
First printing

First printing, March, 2015.

Also by Michael C. Keith:
If Things Were Made To Last Forever; Collector of Tears; Everything is Epic; Sad Boy; Of Night and Light; Hoag's Object; And Through the Trembling Air; Life is Falling Sideways; Norman Corwin's 'One World Flight' (with Mary Ann Watson); The Radio Station; Sounds of Change (with Christopher Sterling); Radio Cultures; The Quieted Voice (with Robert Hilliard); The Next Better Place; Dirty Discourse (with Robert Hilliard); The Broadcast Century (with Robert Hilliard); Queer Airwaves (with Phylis Johnson); Talking Radio; Waves of Rancor (with Robert Hilliard); Voices in the Purple Haze; The Hidden Screen (with Robert Hilliard); Signals in the Air; Radio Programming; Global Broadcasting Systems (with Robert Hilliard); Radio Production

All rights reserved.
Printed in the United States of America.
No part of this book may be reproduced
in any manner whatsoever without written
permission except in the case of brief quotations
embodied in critical essays and articles.

Cover Photography by Glenn Bowie

Cover Design by Bodhi

Bio and Back Cover Photograph of Mr. Keith by Lee Nadel

ISBN: 978-0-9960599-4-7

Library Of Congress Control Number: 2015933535

A COLD RIVER PUBLICATION

Cold River Press
11402 Francis Drive
Grass Valley, CA 95949

www.coldriverpress.com

Author's Note

Most of the stories in this collection first appeared in the following publications: *The Lowestoft Chronicle, Separate Worlds, The Literary Yard, McStorytellers Journal, The Fear of Monkeys, Iron Gall Review, The Penmen Review, Blue Hour Magazine, The Legendary, The Smokebox Journal, Short Humour, The Commonline Journal, The Quail Bell Magazine, The Literati Quarterly, Former People Review, The Greensilk Journal, Calliope Journal, The Zodiac Review, Specter Magazine,* and *Grey Sparrow Journal.*

I cannot imagine the courage and patience it took my readers—Christopher Sterling, Nicki Sahlin, and Susanne Riette—to comment on the over 200 stories I've penned in the past half decade. Now that's what is called staying power. It is my profound hope that you generous and talented people continue to *stay.*

Table of Contents

Snow Job 13

Children of Divorce 17

Beauty Marked 19

Incognito 23

And Now, Ladies and Gentlemen, "Solipsistic Man" 29

Caricatures 31

In the Age of Suspicious Objects 37

Dear Daddy 41

The Ostinado Phrase 47

Trampled by Elephants in Thailand 51

Padre Lamente 61

Mixology 65

The Late 69

Too Beautiful for Words 73

Smoke and Mirrors 75

Virtual Scenes 81

Our Secret Place 85

Table of Contents

Undercurrents..93

A Fish Story..95

The Dress..101

Dead People Ordering Dominos..107

The Flying Flies..111

One Hit Wonder..117

Poetaster...127

Mama's Hurts...129

A Hell of a Day in Heaven..135

Blue Zone..139

Christopher Lee's Eyes..147

Deejay By the Numbers...153

A Fly in the Ointment..155

Consuming Dream..161

Turns Out..169

Stalker 2 Stalker...173

Misinformation...179

Table of Contents

Delusions of Grandeur...181

Metatarsal Prosopagnosia..185

Skin Conditions..189

My Anxiety Journal..197

The Humane Thing..205

The Near Enough...209

The Long and the Short of It...215

The Window On His World...221

Eyes of the Beholders..229

Burning Desires..233

Tuna Melts...239

Nailed..241

Somewhere Out There...245

Finding Poetry on Mars..251

The Valet..257

Life's Priorities..263

Author biography...265

So near and yet so far.
— Lord Tennyson

Snow Job

*This trade of hers—I don't know, can't be sure
But there was something in it, tricks and all!*
— Robert Browning

The dramatic change took less than 48 hours. The two feet of snow that had fallen on downtown Hartford was plowed into mountainous piles that took on the appearance of coal mounds.

Connecticut's very own Black Hills, moaned Stacy Willard, as he headed to his dental practice. *Why does anybody with half a brain live in this climate when summer is just a plane ride away?* He could not have imagined that practically everyone in the endless line of cars ahead and behind him was thinking the very same thing. Indeed, the overwhelming majority of the northern city's inhabitants were suddenly suffering from extreme depression, due to the profound bleakness of the season. *Why do we subject ourselves to this God-awful experience when we don't have to?* What's more, many began to make serious plans to forsake the dirty snow and icy cold and move to Florida. Those clinging onto the lower social and economic rungs of the population remained unaffected by the sudden compulsion to flee south.

In the coming days, the airport, train station, and bus depot were clogged with sun seekers. The main highways stretching from Hartford to Orlando became a virtual parking lot of cars, trailers, and moving trucks jammed with family belongings. Over 100,000 soon-to-be former Nutmeggers were on their way to a new life ...

albeit, slowly. None had plans to ever return to the wasteland of New England winters.

"Why didn't we think of this before?" asked Silvia Willard, as she and her husband eagerly packed their belongings into a U-Haul preparing to start their trek to milder weather.

"I guess I've always thought about moving away from here, but then it just hit me out of nowhere that I . . . *we* could. Of course, I never thought the whole town would get the idea at the same time. Now that's kind of amazing," replied Stacy.

Only a handful of Hartford officials complained that the mass exodus was going to throw the city into chaos. The mayor and most of the city council did not express similar concerns, but only because they, too, were about to leave.

* * * * *

Kirk Bellamy, who represented several of the city's poorest districts, called the mass evacuation a "blatant crime against the poor and underprivileged."

"All you rich white folks care about are yourselves. Don't matter to you that the less fortunate are left behind to freeze their ass off. But that's okay, we'll be better off without you."

And so they were, because shortly after the "Great Departure," as it came to be called, the quarter of the population left behind took up residence in the nicer homes of those who had migrated to Florida. The long-suffering citizens of the city also filled many of the positions that had formerly been occupied by members of the more advantaged classes. Things in the city eventually returned to as close to normal as possible given the dramatic loss of population.

* * * * *

The tens of thousands who had fled Connecticut for warmer climes eventually settled throughout the Sunshine State. They soon learned how their former city had adjusted to their departure and gradually began to wonder why so many of them had simultaneously arrived at the decision to leave Hartford.

"It's like we were mass hypnotized and then instructed to move," observed Silvia Willard.

"Yeah, it does seem really strange that everybody wanted to move here all at once. It was like we were under some kind of spell," replied Stacy, starring out at Biscayne Bay. Still, I'm glad we're here though. Never want to see the mountains of polluted snow again."

"Me neither. I just couldn't go back to that, even if we have to work here at Wal-Mart. Better that than . . ." mumbled Silvia, losing her train of thought as a pelican landed a few feet away.

* * * * *

The newly elected mayor of Hartford, Kirk Bellamy, and members of the reconstituted city council were assembled backstage at the Civic Center. They were ready to launch a weekend of gala celebrations recognizing the revolutionary changes that had so significantly improved the fortunes of Hartford's remaining citizens. On cue, Bellamy and the other city officials walked out onto the stage before an overflowing crowd of cheering supporters.

"Ladies and gentlemen, welcome to the start of the People's Festival. We have come a long way in the last several weeks, and we have much to be thankful for. Most of all we are thankful for the Great Departure. Without it, we'd still be stuck in our miserable slums and dead-end jobs. Of course, none of this would have been possible without the extraordinary gift of Madame Obeah. So let's all give her the welcome she so richly deserves."

Shanique Obeah emerged from the right side of the auditorium stage. She was a mesmerizing image in her brightly colored kanga and glistening headwrap that created a saintly halo.

"Thank you Madame Obeah for your powerful juju. It has worked far beyond our wildest expectations."

Obeah smiled and bowed gracefully to the adoring and grateful audience.

When the roar of the crowd subsided, Obeah spoke, "My children, I have given you only what you were wrongfully denied."

Children of Divorce

I balanced all, brought all to mind,
The years to come seemed wasted breath,
A waste of breath the years behind.
— W.B. Yeats

When he awoke from his afternoon nap on the front porch, he immediately noticed that the house was terribly askew.

"Lord, will it ever settle down?" he groaned.

The facade was leaning at a perilous angle and the roof pitched in a drastic southerly direction. Meanwhile, the dormers tipped both east and west threatening to topple. Every door assumed its own hazardous position, and the windows went this way and that about to shatter.

As he stood up, he landed on his backside, yelling "What's up?"

"No!" shouted his wife from below. "I'm down. You're up."

"Here we go again," growled their landlord. "Your lease specifies that you must keep your house in order, and this is anything but. Look at what you've done! What do you have to say for yourselves?"

"We're sorry, but it's very hard to keep things together when we're both from broken homes," replied the distraught tenants.

Beauty Marked

Here Files of Pins extend their shining Rows,
Puffs, Powders, Patches, Bibles, Billet-doux.
Now awful Beauty puts on all its Arms;
The Fair each moment rises in her Charms,
Repairs her smiles, awakens ev'ry Grace,
And calls forth all the Wonders of her Face.
— Alexander Pope

Little Abby Sinclair was not fully satisfied with her looks, despite the fact that everyone said she was very pretty. In her eyes, however, she lacked that singular defining feature that would place her in the category of the world's most glamorous women. Madonna, Cindy Crawford, and Angelina Jolie all had one, and she was determined to have one, too.

To her great joy, Abby believed she'd found the way to address her one physical shortcoming. She immediately went through several popular movie and fashion magazines to determine the best place to add the emblematic spot. After studying countless photos of stars and models, Abby concluded that the speck would show off best just above her lip. With that in mind, she went to her bathroom mirror and prepared to transform her appearance... and her life.

Two dabs of the black Magic Marker against her supple skin, and she became the person she had so desperately wanted to be. *I'm Marilyn Monroe. The most beautiful girl at Darby Middle School,* she thought, staring at herself with uncontained delight.

Look at me! Look at me! she squealed.

"Come down, Abby. The school bus is coming, honey," shouted her mother from the foot of the stairs leading to the second floor bedrooms.

Abby quickly wiped the mark from her face, leaving a red blotch in its wake. She knew her mother would never let her out of the house with it.

"Don't run. The bus is just getting here," said Pam Sinclair. "Have a good day, sweetie pie. Get A's, okay?"

Abby located an empty seat in the rear of the bus. There she reapplied the felt pen to her upper lip. As she did this, the bus hit a pothole, causing her hand to move. The result was a slightly larger mark than she had planned on making. She was not aware of this until her classmates brought it to her attention.

"What's that on your face?" asked her best friend, Mary Parker.

"Looks like a bug," declared Dennis Copland, snickering.

"It's not a *bug*. All the movie stars have one."

"Well, it does look like a bug," observed Sally Butler, squinting as she took a closer look.

"Hey, guys, look at bug face," shouted Dennis.

"Shut up!" yelled Abby, placing her hand over the object of their ridicule.

"Bug face! Bug face!" chanted several boys, prompting other kids in Abby's class to join in.

"It's a beauty mark! You dopes!" blurted Abby, running from the classroom just as her teacher arrived.

"What's the matter, Abby?"

"I have something on my face. I'm going to the lavatory to wash it off."

Abby stood before the bathroom mirror and wiped the ink from her face with a damp paper towel. *It does look like a bug*, she thought, tears welling up in her pale green eyes. *Why do they call it a beauty mark? How come the stars have them? It's stupid . . . I'm stupid.*

Instead of returning to her homeroom and facing the mockery of her schoolmates, Abby left the school and began walking home. On her way, a car pulled up with a man inside, who reminded her of Justin Bieber . . . but older.

"Hey, beautiful girl, you want a ride?" he asked, pushing the passenger side door open.

Beautiful, thought Abby, flattered. *He thinks I'm beautiful.*

After only a moment's hesitation, she climbed into the car, and it sped off.

Incognito

The knowledge of man is as the waters, some descending from above, and some springing from beneath; the one informed by the light of nature, the other inspired by divine revelation.
— Francis Bacon

As was his custom, Rabbi Avner Banheim climbed from bed before sunrise to begin his long day. But this was no ordinary morning in the life of the fifty-two-year-old, because he was overcome by the urge to embrace Jesus Christ. He had no idea why he felt this way, but he sensed it was crucial to do so. *I must convert the shul to a church and tell my people to appear as Christians, with bibles and rosaries*, he told himself. *I must do this. But why? But why?* he questioned, about to don his yarmulke, but then taking it and other objects that defined him as a rabbi and Jew to a hiding place. *My members must heed my request*, he told himself with growing intensity. *How will I tell them that they must do such a strange thing when I myself do not know why?*

Rabbi Banheim immediately called a meeting of his temple's congregants and with great trepidation attempted to convey to them what he felt they must do. He conceived of a plan that might give substance to his bizarre request.

"We must replicate a Christian church service to help us

obtain a broader view of the world's major systems of worship. To do so will enhance our appreciation of Judaism."

As he feared and expected, his words were greeted with skepticism and confusion.

"This seems a very strange exercise, Rabbi," commented one member of the more than 50 assembled in the modest structure.

"Yes, a sacrilege to perform the rites of Goyim in our temple," observed another.

"Without an appreciation for other beliefs we cannot fully appreciate our own. Please, I implore you as your rabbi to participate in this recreation. It has come to me on this day that it is crucial for us to do so."

"But why, Rabbi?" blurted several members.

"I cannot explain other than to say I awoke this morning with a belief that to act as Christians in the days ahead would benefit us beyond all other things. I have been your rabbi for a long time. Have I not always had your best interests in my heart and actions?"

"Yes, Rabbi Banheim," said the eldest member of the shul's congregation. "You have been our leader, and we will do as you wish now. What is it we must do to appear as Nazarenes?"

"Remove all objects of our faith and replace them with the sacred relics of Christianity. The temple must appear as a church, and you must look like gentiles worshiping their God."

"When must this conversion take place, rabbi?"

"Right away. We must act with great alacrity. I believe our well-being depends on it."

* * * * *

Over the next two days, members of the temple gathered objects of the Christian religion and brought them to Rabbi Banheim, who in turn used them to replace the Judaic icons that adorned the altar of the small synagogue. On the morning of the second day, the rabbi had awakened with the conviction that the reenactment of a Christian service must occur the very next

Sunday. He instructed his followers to be at the converted temple then and to make certain they behaved as Christians would on their Sabbath.

In the days that followed, Rabbi Banheim's apprehension grew, and he feared for the lives of his adherents. *I pray to You, O God, from this most confused place and I entreat Your help in these terrible moments,* repeated the cleric to himself, as he rehearsed a Christian sermon.

He listened to his radio and despaired over the news he heard. That the world behaved in such a monstrous way in 1938 depressed him. *So modern yet so barbarically primitive,* he thought, and then he realized what had impelled him to do the things he had. *Yes, that is it. Thank you, God, for your mercy.*

* * * * *

On Sunday, as directed, members of the temple appeared in the reconstituted house of worship with their prayer books. Rabbi Banheim stood at the altar and instructed his flock to turn to Psalm 27:4-5.

"Please read along with me," he said, detecting the sound of vehicles approaching outside.

> *One thing have I asked of the Lord, that will I seek after: that I may dwell*
> *In the house of the Lord all the days of my life, to gaze upon the beauty of the Lord and to inquire in his temple . . .*

As the psalm was being read, Banheim could see military vehicles pull up from a rear window. A soldier climbed from the lead car and peered inside of the building. After a moment, he turned and walked away. Banhiem heard the soldier's voice above those of the worshippers.

"This is not a synagogue! It is a church with good Christians praying. We have the wrong place. Move on. We will find the Juden, and they will rue the day."

"Heil Hitler," bellowed his waiting troops, who then departed, as the congregation completed reading from their missals.

For he will hide me in his shelter in the day of trouble; he will conceal me under the cover of his tent, he will lift me high upon a rock.

"Amen," said the Rabbi, exhaling deeply.

And Now, Ladies and Gentlemen, "Solipsistic Man"

I've cast the actors in the play I've created,

the characters in the world I own,

So why do I let them upset me

and make me feel alone?

* * * * *

As Acts One, Two, and Three unfold,

they are mine to direct and rule,

To show the world my cleverness,

and not that I'm a fool.

* * * * *

Do I not control the setting?

Can I not affect their schemes,

So the audience will see me as I am,

the star of every scene.

Caricatures

Drawing is the true test of art.
— J.A.D. Ingres

Year after year, Maurice Lucerne set up his wooden easel on the narrow streets of Paris's Left Bank and painted caricatures for tourists. It was how he made a living, but he had grown terribly tired of dealing with his customers. They had become boorish and tedious to him. Regardless of their gender, nationality, or age, they all behaved in the same fatuous ways as he began sketching them with his pastels. They would giggle self-consciously or make silly faces before settling down. It was often in those initial moments that Maurice identified what he wanted to highlight on canvas—furrowed brows, hoary lips, bulbous nostrils, dangling jowls, elephantine ears, crooked teeth, puckish grins, imperious scowls. There was always a singular feature that defined his subjects and set his chalk to motion.

What annoyed Maurice most about his profession was having to make his subjects look funny—but always in a *cute* way. People ultimately wanted to look appealing no matter the nature of the art form. Men and women, and even children, had low tolerance for appearing less than attractive. The world was a vain place, concluded Maurice. Customers didn't mind being the source of a few chuckles as long as the chuckles were of the kind that kittens chasing a string might inspire.

The sketch artist awoke one morning in a particularly ornery mood and there and then decided he was finished painting pictures that ultimately complimented and pleased. *Were not caricatures intended to exaggerate a person's facial characteristics in order to create a comic or grotesque effect?* thought Maurice. *Well, no more damn cute. I've had it with that. I'll go for the grotesque from now on. Maybe that will keep me from going out of my head. Let these tourists see themselves as I see them. I'll capture on paper their true essence. How satisfying that will be.*

* * * * *

Maurice's first customer of the day was an older woman. She was cajoled into sitting for the artist by what appeared to be her two adult children. After considerable resistance, she agreed to be sketched.

"Well, okay. If it's so important to you, I suppose I can do it. But these things are intended to make one look silly, and I don't care to look sillier than I already do," balked the woman, who gave Maurice a look akin to a warning.

A dark mole on the woman's lined cheek caught Maurice's attention immediately. *Voila!* he mused, fumbling through his pastels for a particular color. He went to work and in twenty-minutes he had finished. The result depicted the mole as many times larger than it actually was. In fact, it dwarfed the size of the woman's prominent nose, extending the defect to her upper lip.

"*Fin,*" announced Maurice, displaying the painting to his subject and her entourage.

The woman let out a loud gasp of disapproval.

"What is that? How dare you draw me like that? It is not *me*! My mole is tiny," protested the customer.

"This is an outrage!" blurted her son, while his sister appeared dumbfounded by the whole thing.

"It is how I see you as an artist. That will be 10 Euros," said Maurice, his hand extended.

"I will not pay for this atrocity," replied the young man.

"If you do not, I shall call the gendarme. You agreed to have me draw the good lady. In fact, you insisted. Pay me or incur the consequences."

Flustered, the man tossed a bill at Maurice and escorted his women away.

"Do you not want the painting, sir?"

The young man turned and grabbed it from Maurice's hand.

"Yes, to burn it at the first opportunity!" he growled.

* * * * *

Less than an hour later, Maurice was hired to render a portrait of an overweight tourist. The man spent several minutes combing the few strands of hair he had left before signaling Maurice that he was ready to be sketched.

Un homme moche, thought Maurice, studying his subject. *I will draw you as you truly are,* Cochon grand. Maurice gave the man the snout of a hog with a large, half-devoured sausage protruding from his salivating jaws.

"For you, sir," said Maurice, showing the sketch to his customer.

The rotund man looked mortified as he stared at the caricature. After a moment he spoke.

"You are a very cruel man," he bellowed.

Again, Maurice demanded his money, threatening to fetch the police if he wasn't paid.

"You are no artist. You are a fraud . . . a monster!" proclaimed the man, handing Maurice his fee.

"And this is yours, my good man," said Maurice.

"*Oui,* I will take this *thing* to line the bottom of my birdcage," replied the indignant customer, stomping away with his caricature.

* * * * *

Maurice had no further customers until late in the day when he was about to return home. Before him stood a woman with a child whose head drooped to one side, indicating a severe affliction.

"Please, monsieur, draw my pretty little girl," said the woman, imploringly.

Maurice was conflicted. *What can I do with this poor soul?* He then began to draw the child as her mother gently held the girl's head to keep it from shaking. Unlike with the other caricatures he had made that day, Maurice took great pains with the sketch, spending the better part of an hour on it. The result was inspiring.

"*Madam*, I hope this pleases you. It *is* as she *is*," said Maurice, presenting the picture to the woman.

"Thank you, sir. It is wonderful," replied the woman, holding the drawing close to her daughter's face. "See, my darling. This is *you*. This is *really* you."

The grateful woman handed Maurice twice the amount of his fee and departed happily.

That night Maurice thought of the handicapped child and how he had been sketching his other clients so cruelly. *It is wrong to hurt people when you can make them happy. I will not do it again,* he swore to himself, suddenly feeling renewed interest in his vocation.

* * * * *

As Maurice set up his easel on the Boulevard Saint-Germain the next morning, the young woman with the sick child he had sketched the day before reappeared. Maurice was shocked to see the handicapped girl sitting with her head upright in her wheelchair.

"Dear sir, my daughter was transformed by your drawing. Last night I placed it in front of her while I was in the kitchen preparing supper. When I returned, her head was no longer bent and she was smiling so beautifully. Look at her. It is a miracle. You have done what no doctor could. You have given her such happiness. Thank you from the bottom of my heart."

Tears of gratitude fell from the woman's eyes as she went on her way. *Impossible. How can this be?* Maurice thought, watching the pair as they vanished down the busy boulevard.

No sooner had they left when two figures emerged from the

Metro entrance across from Maurice. One had a grotesque mole covering half of her face and the other had a nose like a pig. Seeing his easel, they moved quickly toward him.

"*Aidez-moi,*" whimpered Maurice, as he began running from his former models.

In the Age of Suspicious Objects

But there's nothing to equal, from what I hear tell
That moment of mystery.
— T.S. Eliot

British Airways flight 239 bound for London from Boston lifted off of Logan Airport's tarmac at exactly 7:15 PM. The flight was rarely off schedule, and BA prided itself on that fact. Passengers nestled into their seats for the seven-hour transatlantic voyage. An hour out, flight attendant Marge Coughlin was fetching an extra pillow for a man in Business Class when she noticed a small box in the same overhead storage compartment. She hesitated before touching it, and when she finally did, she quickly removed her hand from the object, believing she heard a sound emanating from it. *Oh, my God, a bomb!* she thought, her heart beat quickening.

Coughlin immediately called the flight deck and reported the suspicious device. "A funny whirring sound is coming from it, Captain. What should I do?"

The pilot turned the controls over to his first officer and headed through the cabin to where the strange object had been discovered.

"Okay, Marge, we're turning around. Don't move the box, and close the overhead door. Make sure no one gets near it. It may or may not be an explosive, but it certainly looks suspicious. Did you check with the other flight attendants to make sure it isn't theirs?"

"Yes sir, no one has ever seen it before."

The Boeing 777 captain informed Logan Airport that he was returning because of an unidentified object on the plane. He then announced to his passengers that a minor technical issue was forcing him to take them back to their point of origin.

"Goddamn thing's probably on a timer and could blow at any moment," he said to his co-pilot.

"So you think it's a bomb, Captain?"

"Not sure, but when in doubt, it's passenger safety first."

In slightly more than an hour, they were back on the ground in Boston and the plane had been safely evacuated.

* * * * *

Immediately after the deplaning of the last passenger, the State Police Bomb Squad removed the suspicious object and took it a safe distance from the terminal and other planes in order to detonate it.

The head of the bomb squad, Lance Burbeck, arrived on the scene to give the okay for the disarming of the object. But when he took a close look at it, he ordered his team to stand down.

"Holy crap! It's a Victorian Komet Music Box," he shouted, delighted.

"What sir?" asked Lieutenant Miller, Burbeck's second-in-command.

"This is a very rare and valuable music box. I've been looking for one of these for years. I'm sure it isn't rigged to explode. Nobody rigs up something worth thousands to blow up. We'll take it back to the evidence locker, and when nobody claims it, I will."

"Sir, we can't do that until we know it isn't dangerous."

"Oh, for Christ's sake, Miller, I'm telling you it isn't a bomb. Hold on."

Chief Burbeck bent over the box and lifted it.

"Sir, be careful! It may go off. Everybody back up!" shouted Miller, who quickly backed away himself.

"Chill, guys. I'm telling you this is an antique, and you've heard the phrase *finders-keepers*? Well . . ."

Burbeck opened the top of the box and held it high in the air. "Yeah, a bomb . . . *sure*," he laughed.

Wonder why it isn't making music, he was thinking, just as a blinding light flashed and his body was reduced to charred fragments.

* * * * *

Three months later, Burbeck's widow received a package in the mail from British Airways. It read:

> *Dear Mrs. Burbeck, We have learned that your beloved late husband collected music boxes, and in his cherished memory we have acquired the one he had long been hoping to add to his collection. Please accept it as a gift of remembrance for you and your daughter. Sincerely, Myer Johnson, CEO.*

Mrs. Burbeck looked at the gift warily for several minutes and then very gingerly placed it in the trash. The following Thursday the barrel was picked up by the garbage removers.

"Hey, Charlie, I dug this out of the trash. Looks expensive, man."

"Open it up," said his cohort.

A clicking sound came from the box, followed by a rendition of the *1812 Overture*.

"Damn, that's sweet music. Ain't that what they play with the fireworks on the Fourth of July? Why the heck would someone throw it out?"

Dear Daddy

Revenge is a kind of wild justice.
— Francis Bacon

Doug Barren pressed his mother about the identity of his birthfather for months before she very reluctantly told him. It was the most devastating revelation of his young life.

"I was raped at work . . . in the parking garage. You were born 9 months later. I didn't want you to ever know that, but you've been insisting I tell you. And I can't lie to you about what happened."

"So my real father was a rapist? Oh my God! Who is he? Did he get caught?"

"Yes, they arrested him, and he was sent to prison for 5 years."

"Five years for doing that to you? He should have been hanged."

"Well, you're here because of it, so a really bad thing turned into a really good thing."

"I can't believe it. I was born because of a violent crime? Jesus, how do I wrap my mind around that? I feel creepy . . . *dirty*. My whole life seems weird now. Like I don't deserve to be here . . . *shouldn't* be here."

"Look, honey, it has *nothing* to do with who *you* are, so please try not to dwell on it."

"How can I not do that, Mum? You just told me that I'm the result of a sexual assault."

"You wanted to know who your natural father was . . ."

"*Natural?* Ha! That's a good one. A sick crime and I'm here. Great legacy, huh? Where does dear old *Daddy* live now?"

"Why? It happened nearly two decades ago, and he paid the price. And I've got a beautiful son. Please be at peace with it. I am, Doug."

"So tell me his name. I have a right to know that."

"If I do, I want you to *promise* me you'll forget about the whole thing and never do anything silly."

"No, I can't promise that, Mum."

"Then I won't tell you. I don't want another tragedy on my hands."

"Fine, then don't," fumed Doug.

* * * * *

Doug stop pursuing details with his mother and set out to find the name of his biological father on his own. It was not long before he discovered what he was searching for. The newspapers told the full story. The first published report from two decades earlier conveyed the following:

A young woman was attacked in the parking facilities of the McCoy and Franklin Company in Beresford. The victim sustained minor injuries and was taken to hospital for treatment. The suspect is still at large.

Three days later, the local broadsheet revealed that the assailant had been caught.

Lamont Gilmore, 21, of Covington has been arrested and charged with the rape of a young woman in Beresford last Tuesday. The accused has no previous arrests and was an exemplary student, according to his solicitor. A trial date has been set.

Continuing his search, Doug found this statement in *The Daily Echo*:

Lamont Gilmore of Covington has been sent to Oxfordshire Gaol to serve out his sentence for an attack on a Beresford woman. The victim has reportedly moved to London.

Lamont Gilmore, muttered Doug, as he searched the telephone directory for the name. There was no such person listed in Covington now. He then checked the Beresford directory and again found nothing. Finally, he went through the phone books of adjacent towns. With only one directory of the surrounding communities remaining, Doug came upon the name he was so desperate to find in the Brixham directory.

We'll have to pay 14 Wollington Lane a visit, he thought, tearing the listing from the White Pages and placing it in his shirt pocket. *Bet you'll be glad to see your son . . . or maybe not. I'll be really glad to see you and maybe get a little more justice for what you did to Mum.*

* * * * *

On his day off from his new job at Alphagram Technologies in Trowbridge, Doug drove to Brixham and located Lamont Gilmore's address. He parked across from the small, well-groomed cottage and waited. After an hour, he saw a woman and child approach with bundles and enter the house. *Who are they? Your family, Daddy? Did you rape her, too? Maybe the little girl as well?* Doug angrily mumbled. Another hour passed and then he spotted the man he instinctively knew must be his natural father.

The plan he had devised involved confronting Gilmore with a tire iron and smashing his knees after revealing to him that he was the child conceived in the rape of his mother. As Doug was about to execute his plan for revenge, however, an alternative idea occurred to him. It was an act he thought might inflict even more pain on his subject—something that would last as long as his mother's dark memories of her horrible day 19 years earlier. *What if I raped your wife, dear Daddy? How would you feel about that?* Doug slumped down in the car to keep from being noticed.

After a few minutes, he sat back up when he thought the path was clear. *I'll break in when they've gone to bed. I've got rope in the trunk. Tie up Daddy Gilmore and make him watch while I put it to his wife. When I'm done, I'll tell him who I am. He'll never forget that. "In the end, the love you take . . ." you lousy bastard!*

While Doug waited impatiently for darkness to arrive, his mind buzzed with a vast array of thoughts about what his father had done to his mother and how he would avenge the terrible act. But by the time night had arrived, he realized that he could not carry out his plan. The idea of raping someone disgusted him, and he was ashamed he had even thought about it. *I'm not you. I'm far better than that. But you deserve to suffer. I'm not done with you.*

Doug slowly drove home, deep in thought. On the way, he decided to return the following week and take up his original plan to smash the knees of his mother's long-ago tormentor.

* * * * *

By the time the day came for Doug to drive back to Brixham to execute his plan, he had considered a host of new ways to inflict pain on his rapist-father. However, in the end, he felt that destroying Gilmore's knees would guarantee that he would always be reminded of his disgusting crime. *Every time you try to stand or walk, you'll be punished for what you did, and I'll make sure you know who did it to you . . . your little sonny boy.*

Again, Doug parked across from Gilmore's house and waited for his prey to appear. He did not have to wait long. As soon as his mother's offender emerged from his house, Doug clutched the tire iron and went to confront him. He concealed his weapon behind his back as he moved toward 14 Wollington Lane and the object of his loathing.

"Are you Lamont Gilmore?" asked Doug.

"Yes, can I help you?" replied Gilmore.

"I have something for you from Lucille Caufield . . . remember her? The woman you raped 20 years ago."

Just as Doug was about to strike with the tire iron, a young girl ran from the house screaming and pleading.

"Don't hurt my Daddy! Please, don't hurt him!"

And suddenly all of Doug's determination and resolve dissolved, replaced by an overwhelming sense of sadness.

"No . . . no, I won't hurt *Daddy.*"

For a moment both men stared into each other's eyes. Then Doug turned and walked away, dropping the tire iron as he moved.

A split second later, he sensed a figure descending on him from behind and prepared to defend himself. But when he swung around, the pathway leading to Gilmore's house was empty.

The Ostinato Phrase

To my ear they had also a peculiar music.
— Charlotte Bronte

Fierce March winds roared up Seventh Avenue, causing pedestrians to lean forward to keep from being knocked over. Inside the entrance to a parking garage across from fabled Carnegie Hall stood a solitary figure playing a violin. Occasionally, passersby would drop a coin into an open instrument case at his feet. The unusually tall and slender musician would nod his approval while continuing to play.

The compositions he offered were his own and foreign to all those who heard them. Most were improvised, often with curious and unusual results. They were not without merit, but none had been published. Their composer was not interested in material recognition. Content to play his music, he cared little for the trappings of success or fame that might come from his innovations.

Late one afternoon as members of the New York Symphony streamed into the hallowed auditorium across from the obscure instrumentalist, a melody he improvised caught their attention. It was exceptionally unique and exotic and had an immediate and powerful impact on the musicians who heard it. Members of the city's esteemed orchestra paused and peered in the direction of the captivating descant's origin before moving on through the stage door.

By the time the symphony's members were tuning their instruments in preparation for that evening's performance, the extraordinary musical phrase had embedded in their minds, only to manifest itself in the midst of a rendition of Beethoven's Third Symphony. The intrusion was not spurned by the audience but rather enthusiastically embraced by it. Endlessly performed as an encore, it would become the sole piece of music to ever again fill the grand venue.

Those listening to the performance at home or in their cars were equally enthralled by the repeated musical strain. As the hours passed, the inexplicable effect spread. More and more people fell under the spell of the entrancing chords and were completely immobilized by them. Normal activity across the city and nation and soon throughout the larger world ceased as the whole human race become fixated on the arresting notes.

As days became weeks, the only activity occurring on the planet was the mimicking of and listening to the prepossessing divertissement created by the lone Seventh Avenue street minstrel. Everyone had somehow been rendered incapable of engaging in anything else. Routine activities were abandoned. Basic needs were neglected and many people began to grow ill and die. Indeed, and over a far shorter amount of time than might have been expected, the human race perished from the earth . . . but the shard of melody that had caused it played on and on.

* * * * *

Recordings of the narcotizing musical phrase continued to fill the air as the planet was visited by occupants from another world. The benign aliens were responding to the Arecibo message broadcast into space in 1974 and were shocked by what they found upon arriving. The planet's once dominant life form appeared to have simultaneously expired from some unknown cause. What further confounded the alien travelers was an ever-present sound pouring from an array of still-operating audio devices.

After searching the planet unsuccessfully for extant intelligent life, the foreigners departed to pursue the coordinates conveyed in another communique they had received from a different part of the galaxy. It was with great disappointment that the visitors moved on to their next rendezvous, since they had been very keen on making contact with Earth's indigenous species.

Less than a light year away from Earth, the curious sound the extraterrestrials had encountered there suddenly emerged in their own vast brains and took hold of their thoughts, supplanting all others. As had been the case with Earth's inhabitants, the aliens found they could do nothing but listen as their spacecraft sped toward its next destination.

Trampled by Elephants in Thailand

The report of my death was an exaggeration.
— Mark Twain

Ellie Murphy was finally leaving on the trip she had dreamed about her entire adult life. Her fascination with the Far East was born of a desire to track her great-grandmother's roots in a tiny village fifty miles north of Bangkok. She was part Thai and wanted to know more about the relatives her grandmother had talked about so often before her death.

Michelle Murphy had not been as smitten by the urge to learn about her ancestors as was her daughter, and Ellie's father was Irish with only a passing interest in his forebears. Ellie's maternal grandfather had been Irish, too, which accounted for her fair complexion and auburn hair. No one would have ever guessed she was of partial Asian descent. In her heart, however, Ellie felt a great connection to the part of her that was Thai.

"I worry about you traveling to Thailand alone. Can't you find a companion? It's always better to be with someone in new and strange places," observed Michelle Murphy, and her husband concurred.

"Your mom has a valid point, honey. If you were going to Ireland it would be different, but that part of the world is a whole other matter."

"Don't worry, you two. I'm going to join a biking group that is traveling through Thailand, and they're right here in Belmont."

"Well, why didn't you say so? That makes me feel a hundred times better, Ellie. Doesn't it, Phil?"

"God, yes! We've been losing sleep over the whole thing, sweetie."

In truth, however, Ellie was not meeting up with anybody. She hated lying to her parents, but she felt it was the only way to ease their worries about her planned trip to the other side of the planet.

"But you're not really a biker, Ellie," commented Michelle, her expression filling with apprehension all over again.

"You don't have to be, mom. It's not a race. Just touring. We'll be renting bikes there. There are even some old people doing it . . . uh . . . your age."

"Hey, watch it kiddo. We're not old. Just nicely ripened. Sixty is the new 50, you know."

What a wicked web we weave, thought Ellie, excusing herself in order to escape the conversation.

Two weeks later, she flew out of Boston toward her dream destination.

* * * * *

In preparation for her trip, Ellie had researched her ancestral home and found that there was little information about Ban Chai and its 200 inhabitants. She had also engaged a genealogy service for information about her great grandmother's name—Sudarat Phraphasiriat. After spending hours on the Internet, as well as $100 on the ancestral search, all she was able to ascertain was that the name was fairly common in the region in which her great grandmother had lived. *Well, that's better than nothing. Just have to do a CSI when I get there*, Ellie concluded.

As prepared as she thought she was for her adventure, she found the 19-hour plane ride tedious, if not grueling. What compounded her discomfort was the fact that the passenger next to her spent most of the trip snoring and passing gas. Several times Ellie sought refuge in the restroom where she remained for extended periods until someone knocked on the door. *This guy must have overdosed on some kind of bean sleeping aid*, she thought, trying unsuccessfully to cheer herself up. When the plane finally landed, all she wanted to do was take a long shower and sleep away the jet lag, if that was possible.

From home she had booked a room for six days at a two star hotel in Bangkok, called Erawan House. After looking at dozens of affordably priced hotels, she had decided that it looked safe and respectable. Ellie had even showed it to her parents, but they had suggested she upgrade to a three star hotel, offering to pay the difference. Despite their entreaties that she stay at a better place, she held her ground, secretly uncertain whether she had made the right decision.

When the taxi pulled up to the entrance of the modest establishment, she believed she had. At least from the outside, it appeared to be very well maintained. The neighborhood around it was hectic and noisy and exuded what she felt was a positive kind of energy. *This is going to be just fine*, she told herself, climbing from the car she'd hired. To her relief, the inside of the hotel was as pristine as its facade. *So far so good.*

Ellie had no trouble falling asleep, despite the time difference between Bangkok and Boston, and she slept soundly for 14 hours. When she awoke, she was elated to realize where she was.

"Thailand! Oh my God, I'm here. I'm really here. It's not a dream," she squealed rapturously.

She toured the city for two days and soon connected with other visitors to the country, especially a professor of Asian studies from Orono, Maine, who was traveling around the whole of Southeast Asia. During her time in Bangkok, Ellie inquired as to how to reach Ban Chai and learned that a bus ride of two hours would take her there. She had no idea about accommodations in the village and hoped it would not be a problem. Several Internet sites indicated that even in the smallest towns there were places to stay. She prayed that her great-grandmother's birthplace was prepared for visitors. She needed a place to put her head for a night or two, figuring that it would not take longer to gather information about her ancestors, given the small population of the place.

* * * * *

The bus got Ellie to Ban Chai by mid-morning. It continued on to Kamphaeng Phet before returning in the late afternoon for Bangkok. She watched as it drove away. An old man squatted across from where she stood. Before leaving home, she had written several basic Thai words down on a piece of paper, including her great-grandmother's name. Realizing there would be a language issue, she had found a way to translate her relative's name in Thai. She walked across the narrow road toward the elderly man, planning to show him the piece of paper in the hope he might recognize the name.

"Mai," said the man, looking up at her quizzically.

He then pointed to a building next to where the bus had dropped her off.

"*Khaap khoon,*" answered Ellie, reading from her list of Thai words.

The structure she approached had something of an official look compared to others along the street. *Might be the town hall*, thought Ellie, pushing against its weathered door and finding it locked. There was no bell so she knocked. After a moment the door opened a crack, just enough to reveal a face.

"*Sa wat dee khrap.* I am looking for information about my relative," said Ellie knowing it was unlikely she would be understood.

To her surprise and relief, the man seemed to understand her.

"Oh, you speak English . . . great. This is my great-grandmother's name," said Ellie, displaying the piece of paper. The man moved his face close to it. "Of course, she is dead, but there must have been other relatives of hers . . . of *mine* living here.

"No more here," said the man. "No more here."

"Can you tell me where they lived? Do you know what happened to them?"

"They gone."

"Do you know where?"

The man opened the door slightly and pointed upward.

"I'm sorry, I don't understand."

"They die. All gone now."

"Yes, I know my great-grandmother would not be alive, but other relatives might be."

"No, they go . . ." repeated the man, gesturing toward the sky again.

"So no one is here?"

"No, they trampled by chaang."

"Chaang?"

"Yes, chaang . . . *elephant.*"

"Huh? I don't . . ."

"Chaang . . . elephant kill."

Ellie was at a loss for what to say next, and as she stood speechless, the man closed the door. *Okay, now what?* For the next several hours, she approached several of the village's inhabitants with the name of her great-grandmother. But only one responded by repeating what she'd been told earlier— "trampled by chaang."

By late afternoon Ellie caught the bus back to Bangkok feeling frustrated and disappointed. *Trampled by elephants. So, that's it, huh?* By the time she returned to her room at Erawan House, she was in a blue mood and wondering what to do next. *What can I do? There's nothing to do. Trampled by elephants? All of them? That's bizarre.*

* * * * *

With more time on her hands in Bangkok than she expected, Ellie booked a tour to a town on the south Thai coast where she was told a noted festival was taking place. On her way there, to her pleasant surprise, she ran into the female professor from Maine she had met two days earlier.

"So how did your search for your Thai ancestors go," she inquired.

"Not so well, I'm afraid."

"Why?"

Ellie proceeded to tell the woman about her experience in Ban Chai.

"They told you your relatives were trampled by elephants?"

"Yes. I thought that was very strange."

The woman smiled knowingly. "Oh, dear. That is a common reply to strangers, especially Westerners."

"What?"

"People in tiny villages in the country frequently distrust outsiders. When they're asked questions about their town or neighbors, they typically respond with that pat answer. Or if they don't know what to say or don't understand something, they use that phrase. I don't know where it came from."

"No, you're kidding. Really?"

"I'm afraid so," replied the professor sympathetically.

When the tour bus reached the festival village, Ellie was amazed at the massive crowds.

"We should stick together," suggested the professor. "Things can get pretty crazy at these celebrations. The Phukai Elephant Parade is especially popular. People come from miles away to participate and watch the long march of beautifully decorated pachyderms."

As the two women squeezed their way through the undulating crowd, there was a sudden surge followed by screaming.

"Stampede," shouted several people.

Ellie lost her balance and fell. When she regained her footing, she could not find her purse or her companion. It took her several minutes to find shelter, and there she remained until a semblance of calm returned. During that time, she had witnessed several people being carried to what she assumed was a medical center. As she prepared to rejoin the crowd, there was yet another surge, accompanied again by screaming voices, and she quickly retreated to her doorway sanctuary to wait it out.

The chaos continued, on and off, for what seemed hours, and Ellie realized she had missed the tour bus back to Bangkok. After a great deal of effort, she discovered that the only transportation back to the capital city left the next morning. With all available lodging taken because of the festival, Ellie found herself spending the night on a bench in the town's small square.

* * * * *

Back in Boston the Stones had heard about a tragic event involving elephants at a parade somewhere in Thailand. Mrs. Murphy could not but wonder if their daughter had been at the festival, and she became concerned.

"Why would she be there?" reasoned Mr. Murphy. "I mean she didn't say anything about going to something like that, honey."

"It's just my maternal instincts. Several people were hurt there, some died. I'm going to call the Embassy over there just in case."

"Oh, that's really not necessary. It's so unlikely. She's fine. Don't get so upset and let your imagination take over your common sense."

"I guess, but if we don't hear from her when she usually calls at 4 o'clock, I'm going to contact the officials."

Ellie's mother nervously paced the living room floor for several hours waiting for the time she would hear from her daughter. But less than a half an hour before the designated call the phone rang.

"There she is! Early, too," shouted Mrs. Murphy.

But it wasn't. Someone speaking in broken English said he was calling about a Miss Ellie P. Murphy.

"Yes, what's the matter? What about my daughter?" asked Michelle Murphy, collapsing onto the couch.

"Sorry, she die. We have purse and ID card. It how we call you to tell you. She had bad accident . . ."

"How?" choked Michelle.

Mrs. Murphy listened in shock and then let out a wail and dropped the phone.

"What's the matter? What happened?" asked Ellie's father, frantically.

Ellie's devastated parents huddled on the couch and wept.

Twenty minutes later the phone rang again, and this time Phil Murphy answered.

"Hi Daddy," said his daughter.

"Oh my God, is that really you, baby? It's Ellie, Michelle. It's *Ellie*. We thought . . ."

Michelle Murphy all but yanked the phone from her husband's hand.

"We thought you were dead. We just got a call from someone there in Thailand."

"I'm okay, but I've had better days. What did the person tell you?"

"He said you had been trampled by elephants."

Padre Lamente

The ceremony of innocence is drowned.
　　　— William Butler Yeats

I know they'll say I've treated that boy badly. At least that's what they'll believe, because that's how they view things. I'm not going into the details, but you can bet the courts would hang my hide if I were to go on trial. But what I did shouldn't even be a crime. After all, physical affection and intimacy at any age should be accepted as perfectly natural and normal. That's how I see it, and I'm surely not alone in thinking so . . . trust me.

　Hey, I like women, too. Not grown guys, though. I'm no fag just because I'm attracted to young boys. Shit, the Greeks were, too. Their warriors took boys to the battlefield to service their needs, and then those boys grew up and did the same. It was a tradition, for heaven's sake. An accepted practice back then, and we revere the Ancient Greeks, don't we?

　Well, either way, I don't have any intentions of getting caught by the law or attacked by the kid when he grows up and seeks revenge. He shouldn't do that, of course, but that does happen in *this* world. I loved him in my own special way. He should recognize that when he's an adult and appreciate it for what it was, but he probably won't. So there's only one thing left to do . . . get him before he gets me.

He's only a tender 13 now, so I'm not worried about him coming after me. Not yet, anyway. He's so small and passive . . . a baby, really. I'm not all that concerned about him telling anybody, at least not for a while. He's too confused by what I did with him and probably too embarrassed to say anything. But he'll be a different story in a few years. I'll have to plan for the eventualities, I suppose. Isn't that a shame . . . in a so-called civilized society?

Well, he's coming over, and we're going to spend a little quality time together. I bought him a special outfit that he can only wear when he comes to my house. I think he'll like it. He may think it's a little odd, but I'll convince him that it's not and ask him to please put it on just for me. He'll do that. He does what I ask him. He's nice that way. I really do love him.

Oh, there's the doorbell. He's here.

Hi, Tommy, come on in. Well, don't you look cool in that jacket? Is it new?

Who are those men in suits behind him?

Oh, you brought someone with you? Hello, who might you gentlemen be?

Please step outside, sir, and turn around. You're under arrest for indecent acts against a minor . . .

Under arrest! I never did anything like that! That's disgusting! What did you tell these men, Tommy? I thought you loved me.

Mixology

There is something that excites compassion.
— Sydney Smith

Sheila strutted into Mac's gin mill, her musty fox stole hanging from her shoulder.

"Hey, Sheila, where you been? Haven't seen you in a few," said Scotty, the barkeep.

"Oh, you know, here and there. A girl's got to stay busy."

"Doin' what, hon?" asked Scotty, with a knowing wink.

"Never you mind. It's not that interesting after you've done it a while."

Scotty placed Sheila's regular before her, and she emptied the glass of her favorite 100 proof Scotch in one swift gulp.

"Well, you sure ain't lost your taste for it. You can hammer 'em back. I'll give you that."

"You've never seen anyone like ol' Sheila, eh? So hit me again, Scotty. Had a hard night."

"You keep this up and you're gonna' have a harder day."

Scotty refilled Sheila's shot glass and noticed a black and blue mark under a layer of makeup next to her left eye.

"Looks like you came up short in the ring," he said, pointing to Sheila's face.

Sheila downed her drink and pushed her empty glass in Scotty's direction.

"Really? You got to be kidding me. Another one of those and you'll have a matching bruise after you hit the floor."

"Just do what you're paid to do, Scotty... okay?"

"I ain't paid to kill people, but it's your funeral, lady," said Scotty, refilling Sheila's glass.

"I'm fine. Don't feel a damn thing. You watering down this stuff?"

"Just a little, but not enough to make a real difference," admitted Scotty, with a cagy grin.

"Mac is such a freaking skinflint. Charges more than he should for drinks and then dilutes them. That's low."

"Hey, you know Mac. If he can squeeze a penny more out of something, he'll do it."

"Why do you work for the cheap bastard?"

"Mac's okay. Just tight with a buck."

"Yeah, I like the jerk, too. By the way, where the hell is he?"

"Goes to noon Mass every day."

"That's right. I forgot he's a Jesus freak."

Sheila, swallowed the contents of her glass and again slid it over to Scotty.

"After this one, I'm cutting you off."

"Yeah, right. I'm touched by your concern for my welfare. Keep 'em coming, sonny."

"Look, if you get hurt or someone else because you got all liquored up here, it's big trouble for us. I should have cut you off after your second drink. Never seen anybody slam back four of these and still stay standing."

"You live a sheltered life, Scotty," said Sheila, polishing off her fourth drink.

"Yeah, I never get out of this cave."

"Mac's got you by the balls, hon. You can do better than this joint. How come you gave up the magic act? I remember seeing you over at Ruby's Place a few years back. You were pretty good."

"Got tired of fooling people with cheap tricks. And Ruby got tired of me doing them and dumped me. Couldn't find any work doing old sleight-of-hand routines."

"So now you serve watered-down drinks for Mac. Good career move."

"Hey, it's a living."

"One more, Scotty, and I'll leave. Promise," said Sheila, holding up her empty glass.

"You're crazy. This stuff would knock Godzilla on his ass. Christ, you have a high threshold for booze. You *are* something."

"I am . . . ain't I? Never underestimate the power of a *real* lady, Scotty."

"Okay, this is it! I *mean* it"

"Ahh . . ." mumbled Sheila slamming back her final drink. "Okay, I'm going to my next John . . . er, job."

As Sheila climbed from her stool, she weaved and had to clutch the bar for support.

"Whoa! Okay, maybe I do feel a little bit woozy, but not enough to keep me from doing what I got to. Take more than the swill you serve to put ol' Sheila on her back. At least, 100 bucks," she chuckled and winked.

After she left the bar, a patron who had observed what had occurred questioned the bartender.

"Why'd you keep feeding her drinks? I never saw anybody down that much alcohol in 30 minutes and still be able to walk . . . or move, for that matter."

Scotty began to laugh. "She's fine. Didn't drink what she thought."

"Huh?"

"Gave her ArKay Scotch."

"What's that?"

"It's non-alcoholic booze."

"Why'd you do that, buddy?"

"Keep her from getting in trouble. You got to look out for a gal like Sheila. Besides, she paid a wad of greenbacks for a sawbuck's worth of drinks."

"You're a real saint."

"No, just a former magician."

The Late

I could not see my friend, because he was not there.
— R.H. Barnham

Everyone is late these days. I don't mean *not on time*. I mean late as in *dead*.

On Monday I go to see my old Army friend, Herb Balak. When I knock on his apartment door, his wife answers.

"Where's Herb," I ask?

"He had a heart attack last night . . . died," mutters Mable Balak.

I start to say something, but she shuts the door in my face. Never did like Herb's wife. Nobody did.

Herbie's dead? No, I can't believe it! He was overweight, but Jesus. Oh, I'll miss you, my friend.

* * * * *

Tuesday I take the subway to Queens to visit my former business partner, Ira Shorstein. When I get to his house, there's a black wreath on the door. *Oh shit! Not him, too?* I think. Then the door opens and there he stands. I let out the air I've held in.

"Hi, Misha. Thanks for coming by. Who told you?"

"Told me what?

"That Claire passed away," Ira responds, his eyes the color of fresh lacerations.

"I'm so sorry. She was a nice lady."

She really wasn't so nice . . . another Mable, actually. But I'm not about to tell Ira that. He's in rough shape.

"I'll be moving to my son's in Atlanta. Nothing left up here for me now," says Ira.

Damn, he'll soon be gone forever, too.

* * * * *

Wednesday is my day to meet up with Larry at IHOP. We've been doing this for years. It's always a hoot. I really look forward to it. Larry makes me laugh, and I think I do the same for him. And Oy vey, do I need to laugh.

It's 9:30, and we're always here at 9:00. Strange. Finally, I call his house, and his daughter answers.

"Hey, Rita, where's Larry? I'm here at IHOP, and he hasn't arrived."

There's silence at the other end of the line and then a long, anguished moan.

"Oh, Misha, Daddy is gone! He fell and hit his head in the shower."

I don't know what to say. Three friends dead in as many days? God, I guess that's the way it happens at this age. I hang up after expressing my condolences. When the waitress comes around again, I order a poached egg and coffee. Larry always took his coffee black.

* * * * *

Thursday is my day to play mahjong with Joey Lippshitz. I'm filled with apprehension, thinking the worst. He's the youngest of our group, though, so I expect he'll outlive everybody. When I reach to the senior center, he's there. Whew, thank the stars! He spots me and jumps up. As he dashes toward me with his arms spread wide—his usual way of greeting me—he suddenly falls. I figure he's slipped on something and run to him.

"Joey, you okay?" I cry as I bend down to him.

He doesn't respond, and a crowd begins to gather around us.

"Call 911!" I yell, watching as Joey's face grows pale and then blue.

By the time the paramedics arrive, I know he is gone. They confirm this and cart his body away. I'm in shock. *Too young*, I think, *too damn young. Nobody dies at 70 anymore. It's the new 60, they say. And who dies at 60 these days?*

I think about finding another partner to push around the tiles with, but my enthusiasm for the game is just not there, so I head toward home. The apartment never seemed so empty.

* * * * *

When Friday arrives, my spirits are at an all-time low. All I can think about is the loss of four good friends. Poor Herb, Claire, Larry, and Joey. Gone . . . all *gone*.

I always see Mel on Fridays. *Why bother going down to Katz's Deli?* I tell myself. He won't be there . . . probably dead, too. But, what the hell, I might as well go. Nothing else to do. Who knows, just maybe he'll show up.

Twenty minutes late. And it's not like him. He's Mister Punctual. Forget it. Go home. He's not coming. Don't even call his house. Just more bad news. Poor Mel Simon. Shit, *poor* Misha Holstein!

Thank God the weekend is here. Don't have to meet someone who's not going to show up. Got a hearing aid appointment early Saturday morning. At least *they* won't be dead.

* * * * *

Healthy Hearing calls Misha's phone number. It rings and rings. *Hmm, must be on his way. That's strange. He's never late,* mulls the audiologist. Fifteen minutes pass, and he dials Misha's number again. It rings repeatedly. *Nope, not . . .*

"Hello," answers a groggy voice at the other end of the line.

"Oh! Mr. Holstein?" asks the Healthy Hearing caller.

"Yeah," replies Misha, groping for his glasses on the night table.

"You're *late* for your appointment."

Too Beautiful for Words

Smoke and Mirrors

*Guilt is the price we pay willingly for doing
what we are going to do anyway.*
— Isabelle Holland

Nearly fifty years after the Surgeon General declared smoking a health hazard, the Globe Tobacco Company continued to thrive. The fact that the government's pronouncement had barely impacted the company's bottom line gave its longtime CEO, Joshua Winston, faith that Americans would never stop lighting up, despite years of reports on the dire effects of tar and nicotine.

"It's a good, solid business we're in," proclaimed Winston on more than one occasion at the annual GTC employee summer barbecue. "And there's nothing wrong with what we do. We provide our customers with something they desire. We fulfill a need, and that's what a good product is supposed to do."

At that point in his speech, Winston would invariably enumerate the benefits of cigarettes.

"They're calorie free, and they actually curb the appetite. They help the user relax. Aid digestion. Give our customers something to look forward to. Cigarettes make the user look cool, especially our menthols," said Winston, with a smug chuckle.

At the end of his soliloquy, everyone present would light up in a show of solidarity, and Winston would nod in approbation.

GTC senior product inspector Cary Newton would pretend to smoke, but as soon as he could he would douse his cigarette and pop a mint to rid him of the foul taste. He had once been a smoker, indeed a fairly heavy one, but a prolonged cough had convinced him that the habit was taking its toll. His lungs had soon cleared of the tobacco residue and in the process made him even more keenly aware of the deleterious effects of smoking.

Since joining GTC, Newton had grappled with the idea that he worked for a company perceived as a public health risk by most of the population. It weighed on him that he drew his paycheck from such an enterprise, but the money was good and other job opportunities were few during the decade he'd spent at the company. He had prospected for a position online, but nothing viable had appeared. So he reluctantly remained in the employ of GTC as his remorse and guilt for doing so mounted.

On a number of occasions he had to defend what he did for a living with what few friends he had. In their eyes he was complicit in the manufacture of a deadly product, and he found it hard to disagree, although he tried.

"Look, no one forces people to buy cigarettes. They do it of their own free vwill. It's like blaming car makers for those who die in accidents."

"Not the same thing, Cary. C'mon. Cigarettes are *inherently* dangerous," argued Felix Dubois.

This kind of debate continued between Cary and his cohorts until the wide gulf it created permanently separated them. Eventually, Cary came to believe that his job had destroyed his social life. Except for his coworkers at the GTC plant, he had little contact with people. Even his relatives had become remote, or so he felt. Secretly, Cary knew that it had more to do with his own remoteness than theirs. They had expressed their negative views about his job, but they had not done so as condemningly as had his friends. Still, Cary felt diminished by their attitude over what he did for a living.

"Can't you do something else?" his Aunt had inquired. "Something that doesn't hurt people? You're a smart young man. It must be difficult working for a company that turns people into addicts and then makes them sick and even kills them."

"I would, but I can't find a job that pays what they do. And I've got bills to pay. Besides, I'm just a low level employee. I didn't invent cigarettes. The company will keep doing what it does even if I leave," responded Cary defensively.

"Still, Cary, it really *is* blood money."

The comment had been the last straw for Cary, and for nearly two years he had avoided contact with members of his disapproving family. Had his parents still been alive, he would have had their support, but in their absence he felt very alone.

Blood money, he thought, feeling both anger and despair.

* * * * *

As winter gave way to spring, Cary noticed that he'd developed a cough much like the one that had forced him to stop smoking a half dozen years earlier. It wasn't long before he was fearing that he'd finally developed cancer from his years of smoking—that it had finally asserted itself as he feared it would. He Googled the symptoms and found that a persistent cough *could* be one indicator of the dreaded disease. The website also made it amply clear that a bothersome cough could also indicate many less lethal afflictions, such as the common cold. Despite this, Cary soon convinced himself that he suffered the Big C.

He resisted seeing his doctor because of what he believed would be the grim outcome of such a visit. However, as weeks went on and his coughing continued, he decided to face the bad news. What brought him around was a plan he embraced with great enthusiasm. He would use his diagnosis to advance the cause against tobacco consumption. This would involve informing GTC that he had lung cancer from smoking its product and that he was going public with that news. If he were fired, even better, he thought. Then he would be a double victim of the harmful industry. In that case, he would then stand at the entrance to the facility with a placard outlining his plight.

Dr. Ramsey, Cary's longtime primary care physician, seemed

fairly matter-of-fact about his patient's symptoms, but he did order x-rays to make certain nothing serious was wrong. Cary did not reveal his conviction that he had lung cancer. He was given a prescription for an expectorant and cough syrup and told that his x-ray results would likely be back in a couple days. He'd be called when they arrived.

"If there's anything that needs further attention, we'll get you back here," said the doctor, adding, "But I doubt there will be."

* * * * *

While Cary awaited what he was certain would be bad news, he continued to plot his protest against GTC. Doing so helped ease his anxiety while providing him with some solace—something positive would come of a bad situation. A day after his doctor's visit, he decided to contact his Aunt, his closest relative since the passing of his parents, and let her know what was going on. While she was upset by what he indicated was a certain cancer diagnosis, she commended him on his strategy intended to heighten the world's awareness about the nefarious impact of his employer's product.

"I'm proud of you for taking a stand against those horrible people. They know they're killing folk, and all they care about is the money. It's a despicable business. You're living proof of what happens when you use what they make. They won't like what you're going to do at all, and that's good. I'll let your cousins know, honey. Maybe we'll come and protest with you."

"Thanks, Aunt Pat, but it's better if I stand out there alone. It'll make people more sympathetic to my cause . . . the lone voice of reason in the wilderness."

Two days later, Cary got the call he expected but not the news he anticipated.

"Hello, Mr. Newton. This is Doctor Ramsey's office calling with the results of your x-ray."

"Oh, yes," replied Cary, catching his breath. "I've been waiting to hear the bad news."

"No, it's *good* news. Your lungs appear quite normal, except for some congestion from your cold. I suspect the medicine has already cleared up much of it," said the chirpy voice.

Cary was at a loss for words but managed to thank the caller. He breathed a sigh of relief and then thought about what to do with his plan to confront GTC. *I'll still do it*, he thought. *I don't have to actually have lung cancer. I can say I suffered greatly from the fear that I did have cancer after all my years of smoking. May not be as effective, but I'll still be making an important statement. This is just something I need to do, job or no job.*

He retained his resolve to take action against the cigarette maker when he arrived at work the next day. As he was entering the building, he ran into his boss, Lance Corbett, the director of quality control. Cary was poised to initiate his plan, when Corbett asked him into his office.

"How long have you been with GTC, Cary?" he asked, directing him to a chair in front of his desk.

Cary was thrown by the unexpected question. He was about to let rip with harsh words against tobacco but instead found himself answering Corbett's question.

"Almost ten years?" repeated Corbett, nodding approval. "Well, you've done a great job for GTC, so I'm happy to tell you that you're going to be promoted to assistant director of quality control. Congratulations, Cary. Nice bump up in salary, too. Welcome to management."

Cary was completely stunned by the news and suddenly very unsure about what to do next.

"Smoke?" said Corbett, offering Cary a GTC Menthol Supreme.

Cary hesitated, and then he accepted one. Corbett took a long, luxurious drag on his cigarette and exhaled slowly.

"Life is good, eh, Cary?"

After a moment's reflection, Cary drew deeply on his own cigarette.

"Yeah," he replied, making a large O with the smoke that rushed past his lips. "Life *is* good."

Virtual Scenes

The greater cat with golden eyes
Stares out between the bars.
— Victoria Sackville-West

Walter called his wife at her sister's in St. Paul to confirm that today was the one-year anniversary of the death of their beloved cat, Moses.

"Yes, it was a year ago today, as a matter of fact," answered Bella, thoughtfully. "Lord, it seems impossible that a year has gone by since he died."

"Okay, well I was looking out of my office window toward his grave just now, and . . . well, I don't know how else to say this, but I saw him. I mean, I *see* him right now. He's walking toward the house."

"C'mon, Walt, that's not even funny."

"I'm not screwing around. I see him. Hold on, let me get a closer look out the window."

Walter pressed his nose against the glass and then stepped away catching his breath.

"My God. It's either him or his clone," Walter gasped into the phone.

"How could it be him, for heaven's sake? He's dead, Walter. Are you all right? Anything the matter? Is this just another of your foolish pranks?"

As Walter peered out of his office window, the grey tabby moved closer.

"No . . . *no*! I'm not joking. It totally looks like him. He's just as huge, and he has that funny curlicue design next to his nose. But I know it can't be him. I mean . . . He's on the porch. Let me see if he comes inside like Moses did by pushing the screen door open. I'll call you back."

Walter left his office and headed for the porch. But before he was halfway there, the cat he thought he might be imagining stood before him in the family room.

"Holy crap! Hello there kitty," muttered Walter, stooping to meet the mystery feline's eyes. "Oh God, you look just like . . . "

Without any hesitation the cat walked up to Walter and brushed affectionately against his leg.

"You *are* . . . I mean, that's impossible. Let me check your tag."

Walter took hold of the animal's collar and nearly fainted when he saw the word 'Moses' on the blue medallion that his cat had worn for all of its 14 years.

Mother of God. You can't be Moses. Not possible. Just freaking not possible. But damn if you don't look and act like him. Maybe I'm losing my mind. Let me call Bella back and let her see for herself, he thought and speed dialed her number.

"Hello, again. Can you see me, Bella?"

"Yes, I can. You look like you've seen a ghost. So, did our dead kitty come back from the grave?" snickered Bella.

"He did. Look . . ."

Walter directed his iPhone camera toward the cat standing between his legs.

"Bet you can hear him purring, too."

"Are you kidding me?"

"No, I'm not. Just look for yourself."

"Look at what? I don't see anything but the floor."

Walter moved his cellphone camera to the cat's collar and held the tag close to the lens for his wife to see.

"There," said Walter, confident that she must see it.

"There, *what*? All I see are your feet."

"Now you're the one joking. He's right here. I can see him in the camera."

"Walter, I swear, I don't see anything. Just your slippers. What's the matter with you? You're really acting very strange."

"*Me*, strange? What about you? You really *don't* see Moses? I mean, I don't understand. He's right here. It must be Moses. He looks identical, and there's his tag."

"Did you take the pills the doctor gave you? Or did you take mine again by accident?"

"Yes, I took my pills. I can *feel* him . . . his thick fur, Bella. So I'm not just *seeing* things."

"Well, I don't know what to say. I can't see him, and how could I? Moses died on this day exactly one year ago."

"But . . ."

"Oh, wait . . . Oh my God! What is that enormous snake next to your right foot?"

"Huh? What snake? I don't see . . . "

"Run, Walter! Get away from it before it attacks you."

At that moment, the doorbell rang, and Walter turned answered it. It was Frank Berg, his next-door neighbor

"Hi, Walt. Just came over to . . . Whoa, so you got another cat that looks exactly like Moses?" said Frank.

"Oh, you can see the cat, too?" asked Walter, greatly relieved.

"Of course . . . and that's great. But, man, why'd you get that python, too?"

"Huh? *What* python?"

Our Secret Place

Addresses are given to us to conceal our whereabouts.
— H.H. Munro

On my tenth birthday, my brother, Joel—who is a whole three years older—tells me a secret. He says it's his gift to me.

"Where is it?" I ask, after he says he's found an empty cabin.

But he doesn't answer my question right away.

"Where!" I press, and he tells me that it's on the other side of the mountain from where we live. "Let's go," I say, putting on my shoes.

"No! Hold your horses, Katie, and don't tell nobody, especially not Pa Gil."

"I want to go there, Joel."

"Tomorrow, after we done our chores. So shush about it, okay?"

"Are there ghosts there?" I inquire, delighted by the idea of a haunted house in the far woods

"Maybe," Joel replies, teasing me like he always does. "But we can't go there right now, so don't say nothin'. If you do, I'm gonna say you made it all up. Pa Gil says you do that a lot. 'Member he told you it was like telling lies. So you'll be in trouble if you say somethin.'"

"I won't tell Pa Gil nothin'," I say, and I mean it.

We both hate our step-daddy because he's mean, especially when he drinks the moonshine from his still. Then he beats Mama and hits us when we try to stop him. He's no good, says Mama, but we ain't got no place else to be, so we're stuck with him. Sometimes he touches me funny. I don't like that.

* * * * *

After doing our chores the next morning, we start off to the empty cabin Joel found, but before we're even two steps away from the house, Pa Gil demands to know where we're going, and before we say one little word, he tells us to move a bail of hay out to our heifer, Gertie, in the lower field. He calls us lazy youngins, and spits a gob of chew tobacco in our direction. He's disgusting. I seen him empty his nose on the ground more than once.

As soon as we get Gertie her hay, we start off to the far off cabin again. It takes us most of an hour to get there, and I'm tired from all the climbing up and then back down the mountain. Joel ain't tuckered like I am, 'cause he's really strong. He's got big muscles, but not like Pa Gil. When he grows up he will, and then Pa Gil better watch out.

"There it is, Katie," says Joel, pointing his finger at a dilapidated shack nearly covered up with high grass, shrubs, and vines.

"You said it was nice," I protest, but Joel says he ain't never said nothin' like that.

He's been inside the cabin before and leads the way past a back door that is hanging from one rusty hinge.

"It's better inside," he says.

The floor creaks as we enter, and I expect something horrible to leap out at us any moment.

"C'mon, Katie. Ain't nothing in here but some old furniture. No boogeyman . . . least I don't think so," he says in his spookiest voice.

"Don't do that, or I'm leaving," I threaten. He laughs and calls me a fraidy cat.

"This is our secret place," he declares, and I feel better.

The idea of having our own house to play in helps me get on top of my fear, and soon we're acting like we'd always owned the falling down place.

"There's a bed in that room, but it ain't got no mattress on it," says Joel, nodding toward a door on the other side of what I figure is the kitchen.

After a quick look around the cabin, Joel says to pretend it's our fort and we're being attacked by Indians. After that, I get him to sit at the dusty table while I serve a make believe dinner with our favorite grub—skillet fried biscuits and pork gravy. It makes us hungry for real, so we play something else that don't put us in mind of victuals.

* * * * *

We're having so much fun that we lose track of the hour. By the time we get back home, Mama is upset. She looks mad but not that mad. Pa Gil is on his usual warpath.

"You kids got your Mama all sweat up. Where you been?" he shouts and raises his hand threatening to whip on us.

My brother says we were down by the pond trying to catch us a fish for supper, and Pa Gil asks where the critter is. When Joel says we didn't catch none, Pa Gal says that's too bad because we—meaning my brother and me—are getting nothing to eat for supper. When Mama speaks up for us, Pa Gal tells her to shut up, raising his hand again. He then tells us to go feed the barn animals.

"They get to eat," he says, grinning so his gray teeth make him look even meaner.

Pa Gil's also got a squiggly scar on his face that bulges when he's yelling. Gets all scrunched up and reminds me of a night crawler.

"I wish he would go away," I tell my brother when we're slopping the pig. "I hate him," I add, taking out my anger by whacking the porker right on his snout.

My brother shouts at me for being cruel to the animal, adding, "You do that and you be as bad as him."

"No I'm not. Don't say that," I reply, giving the pig an extra scoop of swill to show I'm sorry. "Wish we had our real Pa."

"He run off when we was little," Joel reminds me. "So he weren't no good neither."

"Still, he was our true daddy, and I bet he never hit nobody," I say.

* * * * *

The next morning Pa Gil says we ain't going nowhere today and gives us extra chores. Joel curses him under his breath and gets a whack in the head when Pa Gil picks up on it.

"You watch your mouth, boy, or get something a lot worse than that the next time."

"Leave him alone!" I shout, and Pa Gil clenches his fist and waves it in my face.

"Keep your hole shut, too, or you'll get the same."

After that he climbs into his old truck saying he'll be back by the end of sunlight. Has some business in town, he claims. We do our chores quickly so we can go to our hideaway and play for a little while. We plan to be back before Pa Gil so he don't go crazy on us.

When we get to the empty cabin, we play what Joel calls 'Castle.'

"Watch out!" he shouts, waving his stick sword at an invisible fire-breathing dragon. "He almost got you, but I killed him before he could eat you."

But our play stops suddenly when Joel spots two people far off heading toward the cabin.

"Quick, hide," Joel whispers, and I point up to the storage loft.

"No, the bedroom closet," he says, and we run to it, squatting down in its darkness.

There's a crack in the door, and we can see out just a little. I jump when there's footsteps nearby, and Joel puts his hand over my mouth so I don't make any noise with it. We hear some voices followed by laughter, and then the strangers are in the bedroom. I'm sure they're here to get us for trespassing, and I can't keep the tears out of my eyes. My brother knows this and holds me tighter.

Suddenly Joel gets all tense, and I can see why. Pa Gil is one of the strangers in the room, and he's with a woman I ain't never seen before. She's got long black hair and big bosoms like mama. They grab at each other, and then Pa Gil spreads an old horse blanket over the bedsprings. The next instant they're both pulling off their clothes, and Joel puts his hand over my eyes. I try to take it away, but he holds tight. The bed starts to creak and the woman begins to moan, like Pa Gil is hurting her. Then he moans loudly, and I'm confused. Is she hurting him, too? I wonder.

Adding to my confusion is the fact that they begin to giggle after all the moaning. Then the woman says she's got to get somewhere, and I can hear her leave. Joel takes his hand from my eyes, and I see Pa Gil raising his coveralls. Then, without no warning, I sneeze, and I can see Pa Gil looking at the closet.

"Who's in there?" he yells, and then yanks the door open. "You little bastards! You been in there all along, ain't ya? Told you not to leave the homestead, didn't I? Get out a there. Gonna teach you what for."

He grabs at us, and we push past him. He chases us into the middle room and we scoot up the shaky ladder leading to the loft. He is on our heels as we run to the other side, and we quickly find ourselves cornered. Just as he is about to reach us, though, there's a loud cracking noise, and Pa Gil falls through the rotted floor. I squeal, even though I'm happy that he ain't got us. We carefully walk around the hole in the floor and climb down from the loft.

"Think he's dead?" I ask, as we stand there looking at his body.

"Don't know," replies Joel. "But it wouldn't be bad if he was."

We move cautiously to where Pa Gil lies, fearing that at any moment he'll jump up and catch us. But he stays still like a shot animal. Joel puts his hand under Pa Gil's nose to see if any air comes out of it.

"He breathing?" I ask, and my brother says he's not sure. "What we gonna do now?"

Joel thinks for a moment and then says we could put him down the well that's next to the cabin. That sounds like a good idea to me.

"If he's dead, it don't matter," says Joel, adding, "And if he ain't, then we'll be rid of him anyways."

It takes all our strength to drag him to the old well. Joel drops a stone down it and we don't hear nothing.

"Must be empty," he says. "Let's lift him up and push him in."

"He's still warm to the touch," I say, but Joel says it takes a while for dead people to get cold.

As we're about to drop him down the well, I think I see Pa Gil's eyes flicker open. It makes me scream, and I jump away, as his body drops down the shaft.

"What's the matter?" Joel asks, and I tell him about Pa Gil's eyes opening.

"Dead people make twitches for a while after they pass on," he assures me.

I wonder how he knows so much about dead people. He's really smart even though we don't go to school much. We both look down the well but see only blackness.

"You think hell is at the end of that?" I ask, and Joel says it sure is for Pa Gil.

"Let's get home."

"What about Mama?" I ask, and my brother says to say nothing, to keep quiet.

"Yeah, it's our secret place," I say, and Joel repeats my words.

Undercurrents

These things are as piffle before the wind.
— Daisy Ashford

My wife says our house is too ancient and needs better insulation.

Not against the cold, she says, but against the spirit that haunts it.

Since we moved in, winds have blown in through the cracks in the walls.

They have left deep wrinkles and dark age-spots on my skin.

She says they are the toxic breezes of decrepitude and age.

I thought her comment was silly and baseless and told her so.

Today I woke up feeling stiff, rickety, and older than yesterday.

"I'm leaving you for a younger man," said my spouse, packing her things.

The next day my wrinkles and age spots were gone.

And so was the turbulence.

A Fish Story

Think where man's glory most begins and ends,
And say my glory was I had such friends.
— W.B. Yeats

The deck of the charter boat was covered with numerous large flapping and gasping Halibut, all of them just reeled in by four fishermen.

"Must have been a school of them," said Harvey Baker, excitedly. "Never seen so many caught at the same time. Amazing!"

"Man, I think you guys caught our quota faster than anyone ever did," observed the young deckhand.

"Guess only Miles came up empty. Fish don't like you, buddy," Baker cajoled his friend.

Miles Cantor was not disappointed over his failure to hook a fish. In fact, he was relieved. The idea of handling the slithery creatures grossed him out. Furthermore, he actually felt sorry for the fish as they frantically gulped the air that could not sustain them. When the fish were knocked unconscious and dumped into the giant cooler, Miles had an overwhelming urge to come to their rescue . . . to try and save them.

"Jesus, that's barbaric! They're living things, and they're being massacred," Miles protested.

"What are you talking about? They're friggin' fish. That's why we're out here. You eat them, don't you?" responded Cary Ellis, heaving the body of his catch into the ice-filled container.

In reality, Miles was no fan of fish or, for that matter, any kind of cooked animal. As he watched his buddies measure their prey to determine who had caught the largest, he wondered why he had agreed to come on the trip. Mostly it was the idea of seeing Alaska, a place he had always found intriguing. However, going fishing had not interested him, and now he knew he had made a mistake joining his friends on the expedition.

"No, I don't eat fish or any other living creatures," responded Miles, exasperated.

"So why'd you come along with us, man?" asked Cary.

"Guess I didn't realize that we'd be butchering all these beautiful sea creatures. Look at them. You can see in their eyes that they know they're doomed. They've been pulled from their natural habitat to be devoured by humans . . . by *you*. We call ourselves a compassionate species and we do this. Pretty pitiful."

"*You're* pitiful, Miles. You knew we were going fishing. It's a sport. Millions of people do it. It's not a crime. Wake up and smell the Halibut, for Christ's sake."

Miles looked at the stack of scaly carcasses in the cooler and noticed that the largest Halibut was stirring among its motionless companions. When he looked closer, his eyes made contact with the creatures. *It's appealing for its life*, he thought. *It wants me to save it. It's in terrible pain.* Miles reached for the sentient sea critter and grabbed it. Though the feeling of its quivering body repulsed him, he lifted it and heaved it overboard.

"Are you crazy, Miles? That was my catch. Biggest one I ever hooked," shouted Ellis, astounded.

"If you love them that much, Miles, maybe you should join them," barked Baker.

"Yeah," agreed Ellis. "Come on guys. Let's help Miles join his *real* friends."

Before Miles realized what was happening, he was being hoisted off the deck and thrown into the Cook Inlet's freezing waters.

As he tried desperately to keep from sinking, he could hear his cohorts laughing back on the boat.

"Go find your fishy little buddies, Miles. Doubt they'll be looking for you," shouted Baker.

"Okay, better throw him a life preserver. Let's reel him in, like we did his chums, or is it chum?" commented Ellis.

"You mean chump," added Baker.

Miles was not a strong swimmer, and the arctic water defeated his efforts to remain afloat. Before the lifesaver could reach him, he sank below the choppy surface.

"Where the hell is he?" bellowed Ellis.

"I can't see him. He's gone under, man?" replied the deck hand, leaping into the water himself.

After several minutes, he was helped back on board without having located Miles.

"Oh, my God! He's drowned. He's gone! What can we do?" whimpered Ellis.

"I've radioed the Coast Guard. You guys are in a heap of trouble, and I'm probably going to lose my captain's license. What the hell were you thinking?" growled the charter boat's skipper.

"We were just joking. Didn't mean for this to happen. He's a friend," protested Baker.

"A hell of a joke! You *killed* your friend."

As Miles was about to lose consciousness, a mammoth Halibut swam up to him and placed its mouth over his and breathed into it. In the same instant, several other fish grabbed Miles and moved him toward shore. Miles sensed that something extraordinary was taking place, but his mind was too addled for him to fully grasp what was happening. By the time he regained lucidity, he was resting against a log back on the coastline.

They saved my life, he thought, incredulously, as he rose and walked toward the pier from which the charter boat had departed that morning.

"What the heck happened to you?" asked the boat lease agent as Miles approached. "Kinda cold in there to be swimming, young fella."

"I fell overboard," answered Miles, not wanting to get his friends in trouble, knowing they did not intend him harm.

"When?"

"Just now."

"Huh? The boat's got to be miles off shore. How's that possible? Got an outboard on your butt? You don't even have a wet suit on. Someone rescue you?"

"Well . . . *sort of.*"

Miles was about to reveal the miracle that had occurred to him, but then thought better of it. *He'll think I'm crazy if I tell him the Halibut saved me. They did save me?* he wondered for a second and again was convinced they had. *Yes, they did. Of course, they did.*

He was taken inside and advised to remove his wet clothes before hyperthermia set in. He draped his shoulders in the blanket he was given without fully wrapping his body in it.

"Darned if you don't even look that cold, son," observed the man.

I'm not . . . I'm not cold at all, thought Miles, smiling knowingly.

"There's your boat now," said the elderly man, pointing toward the horizon. "Looks like it's being escorted by the Coast Guard."

When the boats tied up, a member of the Coast Guard crew was the first to enter the dock's office.

"We got a man overboard under suspicious circumstances, Walt. Found no body. Guy couldn't have survived out there very long," he reported.

Two other Coast Guardsmen then escorted Mile's friends inside. When they caught sight of him, they froze in shocked disbelief.

"Hi guys? How was the fishing?" asked Miles, as if nothing out of the ordinary had occurred.

"How . . . What . . . But . . . ? stuttered Ellis.

Miles gave the group a hard look before answering.

"Some *real* friends rescued me."

The Dress

'Yes: that's how we dress when we're ruined,' said she.
— Thomas Hardy

The sudden death of her youngest daughter so devastated Lily Polowski that she was unable to attend her funeral. Despite being heavily sedated, Lily still suffered from debilitating anguish over the loss of her beloved child. A freak accident on the school playground had taken Debra Polowski's short life. The third-grader had been struck in the head while passing too closely to a moving swing. There was no consoling Lily for months after the death. When she finally recovered some of her former self, she still was far from agreeable company. Most of the time she remained sullen and short tempered, lashing out at her husband and remaining daughter for what she felt was their insufficient level of mourning.

"Neither one of you loved Debra like I did! You're not feeling the loss like me," sniffled Lily.

"That's not so. We loved Debra, and you have no right to say that we didn't," replied Garrett Polowski. "She was my child, too, for chrissakes!"

Young Cela remained quiet, although she wanted to speak

out like her father. Her little sister was dear to her, but she had felt resentment over the greater attention her mother had shown Debra. Just a year younger, Debra always seemed to come first in her mother's life, sometimes to the extent that Cela felt unwanted. In fact, she had wondered if she had been adopted and was quickly assured by her father that she was, indeed, their birth child.

"Then how come Mom acts like Debra is her *real* daughter?"

"Oh, she doesn't think that way, honey. It's because Debra's younger that she pays so much attention to her. She acted that way with you before Debra was born."

"She's only a little younger than me," protested Cela.

Despite her father's attempt to convince her otherwise, Cela continued to feel that her sister received most of her mother's attention and affection. That did not change in the absence of her sister. Her mother's obsession with Debra seemed to grow with each day. It was all she cared to talk about, which further deepened Cela's sense of insignificance. Her father faired even worse. Lily's treatment of Garrett became harsh and vitriolic. She blamed him for Debra's death because he'd been five minutes late picking her up at school on the day she died.

"All you had to do was be on time, and she'd still be alive," Lily had repeated several times a day.

* * * * *

Things took an even darker turn when Lily made a discovery. As she was poring over her departed daughter's things, she found the dress Debra had loved more than anything in the world. Just a week before her untimely demise, her mother had purchased the dress for Debra's forthcoming music recital. It was in that dress that she had asked her daughter be buried. Lily removed the dress from the closet and went yelling for her husband, who sat reading in the livingroom.

"This was Debra's special dress. I asked you to have her buried in it," shouted Lily, as her husband closed his book and placed it in his lap.

"Stop yelling. I did give the dress to the funeral parlor . . . the blue one. Not that one."

"You idiot! You're late picking her up and she dies and you can't even give her a proper funeral? This was her new dress . . . the one she loved most. It's made of taffeta and has an over-skirt of gathered pink netting. The bodice is the same light pink taffeta, but with ruffled short sleeves made from the pink netting. White pearls are sewn along the edge. There's a deeper pink satin ribbon sash at the waist. She looked exquisite in it . . . like Cinderella. She called it her magic dress, and she's not wearing it now. How could you do this to her? The *blue one*, my lord!'"

"It was a mistake. It wasn't on purpose, for God's sake! I thought the blue one was the dress you said to have her wear. It was nice . . . pretty."

"Not as lovely as this one. Are you blind? You've made her very sad."

"She's dead, Lily. How could I make her *sad*?"

"Stop talking like that. You're so cruel. My poor baby is crying in her grave because she didn't have her beautiful dress to wear to heaven."

* * * * *

In the long, dark days ahead, Lily continued to deride her husband until he could no longer stand it and stormed from the house. After two days, Cela began to realize that her father was not returning any time soon, if ever, and her sense of abandonment intensified. The only words from her tormented mother were limited to complaints about her husband, and Cela began to think about running away herself.

The very day she planned to look for her father—she was pretty sure she knew where he would be—and move in with him, Cela's mother came to her with a horrific proposal.

"We'll take Debra's special dress to the cemetery and put her in it. Get ready, Cela. I'll get the shovels in the garage."

Lily placed the pink taffeta skirt and bodice on the couch and left the room. For several seconds Cela stared at her dead sister's cherished outfit, and then she had an idea. She quickly removed her clothes and put on the dress. It fit snugly, but she thought it might have the effect she was desperately hoping it would.

When Lily Polowski returned, her dour expression was instantly replaced by one of unbridled joy.

"Debra, my dearest . . . *dearest* daughter, you're back!" she said, euphorically.

In Lily's eyes stood the beloved daughter she had lost. In Cela's eyes stood the mother she had now regained.

"Yes, Mother," said Cela, fighting back tears. "I'm back. Your *favorite* daughter *is* back."

Dead People Ordering Dominos

Hunger transcend the grave.
— Carl Zajas

We're all in our boxes

Hey, hey, hey . . .

Stored away from the light

Hey, hey, hey . . .

In thick lead containers

Hey, hey, hey . . .

Dark, frigid, airless spaces

Hey, hey, hey . . .

Our 74"x23"x12" crates

Hey, hey, hey . . .

We waste away in silent talk

Hey, hey, hey . . . .

Of things we did when we once lived

Hey, hey, hey . . .

And when we stop no one notices

Hey, hey, hey . . .

Except the guy with our pizza order

The Flying Flies

No good deed goes unpunished.
— Claire Boothe Luce

At an early age, Abdul Karim noticed he could transfer the bothersome floaters that cluttered his vision to another person. It was a great relief to him to find that he was able to do this, since over time he had grown almost blind. His eye doctor had been surprised by his condition, since floaters were uncommon in young people. He suggested Abdul have laser surgery to address the problem, but his parents decided to wait in the hope his condition might improve on its own. When Abdul said he had gotten rid of most of what he called the "flying flies," they believed his malady had corrected itself.

"That is wonderful, my son," said his father, Dabir, "How did you do this?"

"I sent them to other people."

"Really? Well, I suppose that is good, Abdul, as long as no one is hurt."

"I don't think so, Father. They don't seem to notice."

"And who are these people who received your flying, ah . . .?"

"Flies. They're just strangers, Father. No one we know."

"Yes, better they be strangers, Abdul."

His parents were amused by his explanation, knowing that children often have vivid imaginations.

"Well, that is okay. As long as you do not hurt those who get your floaters, I suppose it is fine, Abdul," said Mr. Karim, winking at his wife, Rahiq.

A return to the eye doctor confirmed that Abdul's floaters had nearly vanished.

"That is very unusual. Actually, I've never encountered anything like this. It may have been an infection that caused the floaters . . . something short term passing through his system," observed the perplexed ophthalmologist. "Please bring him back if the condition returns."

To the Karims' great relief, it was never necessary to do so.

* * * * *

Years would pass before Abdul discovered that not only could he transfer his few returning floaters to other people, but in doing so he could also alter the receiver's behavior. How he came to know this was quite accidental. Abdul had sent a floater to a man standing at a bus stop, accompanying it with the words, "To the ground with you!" His playful command had resulted in the man falling backwards onto the sidewalk.

At first, Abdul thought it was a coincidence, so he repeated the injunction. Again, the confused man dropped to the cement. *It is me. Do not hurt him*, he advised himself, startled by his newfound ability. Fortunately, his target was uninjured. When he had another floater two days later, Abdul could not resist the urge to see if he could make his recipient respond to his command once more.

Bark like a dog, he muttered, as he delivered his floater to an elderly woman carrying a shopping bag. The senior howled loudly enough to cause the pedestrians around her to stop in their tracks and stare. *It works. I can actually make people do things when I send them my flying flies*, Abdul contemplated, in delighted amazement.

Abdul began to wonder what else he could do with his extraordinary ability. *Maybe I can make people give me money or do other great things for me. But that would be wrong*, he chided himself, thinking how his parents would react to such selfish thoughts. *No, only do nice things. I'll make people feel good. But how will I do that?*

Abdul decided to order people to be happy, and he initiated his plan by using the same individual he had made fall to the ground at the bus stop the day before. He had noticed that the stranger had a very dour expression on his face before he fell. Something was clearly making him sad, concluded Abdul. He shot his floater at the man, whose face instantly went from a frown to a broad smile. *Wonderful! This is so wonderful! Think of all the good I can do in this unhappy world.*

Abdul anxiously waited for another floater to appear so he could employ his amazing gift once more. *Please come and let me help people from their sadness?* Abdul prayed. When a few floaters finally bobbed into his field of vision, he was excited. He left the house looking for other recipients of his good deeds. As he walked down the busy street in front of his house, he was surprised that everyone appeared in a good mood. He walked on and finally saw a young woman with a crying infant. With an almost imperceptible glance, Abdul transformed the baby's expression into one of glee.

* * * * *

Over the next several days, Abdul spent all of his free time shooting his returning floaters at people who acted as if life were a burden. To see the positive reaction of recipients to his flying flies was immensely fulfilling to Abdul, and he wanted to tell his parents, but chose not to do so. He knew they would think he was just being a silly youngster. *It is my secret. I am doing something wonderful. If they knew what I could do, they would be very pleased,* he assured himself.

Upon returning home after a day of searching for people to make happy, he discovered his mother sitting at the kitchen table and looking very low.

"Mother, why are you sad?" he asked.

"I miss your father. He has gone away on a long business trip and won't return for many days.

"Don't be sad, Mother, I can help you."

"You help me by just being here, Abdul."

"Mother please look at me," pleaded Abdul.

"Of course, Abdul. Do you wish to talk about something?"

As soon as his mother raised her head, Abdul sent his one remaining floater to his Mother's eyes. Like all the others, she instantly responded with a beaming smile.

"Oh, I suddenly feel so much better. How strange. I wonder why?"

"I will tell you sometime, Mother."

Mrs. Karim began to hum happily and rose from the table. She quickly prepared supper, and she and her son had a lovely time exchanging stories of all the pleasurable moments their family had over the years.

Following their meal, mother and son retired to the living room to watch the evening news. It was something Abdul did when his father was away. The first story caught his attention. It told of dozens of people experiencing sudden blindness after first feeling a sense of euphoria. A reporter interviewed the woman with the crying child—who was now sightless—and Abdul immediately knew he had been the source of the terrible mishaps. *All I wanted to do was make people happy with the power I have. I've done something terrible instead,* he thought. And then he suddenly remembered that he had just transferred a floater to his mother.

"What have I done?" he blurted, rushing to his mother's side.

"My sight. There's something wrong, my son. I cannot see," moaned Rahiq, pressing her palms against her eyes.

Abdul's loud wail could be heard far beyond the Karims' residence.

One Hit Wonder

*No gal ever climbed so high
floor by floor to her lover guy*
— Hugh Pompeo

"King Kong Katy" had reached the number four spot on the *Billboard* Top 100 in February 1973. But Hugh Pompeo's followup tune, "Love Car," entered the charts at 89 and then stalled at 73. And that was the last time he'd had a song of note. After two flop albums, he was out of the business. No record company would sign him. He had joined the ranks of The Silhouettes, Domenico Modugno, The Teddy Bears, Stonewall Jackson, The Hollywood Argyles, The Tornados, Jeanie C. Riley, Zager and Evans and dozens of other one hit wonders.

After a few years of playing modest venues, mostly second-rate nightclubs and civic halls, Hugh unplugged his keyboard and took an HVAC certificate course at a local community college. Occasionally, someone would recognize him, but mostly he lived in relative obscurity in Manchester, New Hampshire, just a few miles from the tiny village where he'd grown up.

There were times when Hugh thought about reviving his music career, but common sense decreed otherwise. He knew the prospects were poor that he'd ever succeed again, and by the late 1980s, he had a wife and two young daughters to consider. So the notion of going back on the road struck him as remote, if not inconceivable. He valued his family greatly and did not want to disturb what had become a largely fulfilling existence.

Over the years, however, Hugh had quietly dabbled in song writing, eventually gathering enough material for what he thought would make a good album. He'd squirreled away enough money to rent a local recording studio and went to work. His results met with mixed reviews from his friends and wife. Though his voice remained strong, they felt the CD's potential to find a big audience was low. The problem, as they saw it, had to do with the songs Hugh had composed.

"You sound great, Pomp, but the songs sound . . . well, kind of dated," observed his best friend, Todd.

"Yeah, honey, the music isn't exactly what's hot right now. It comes across as too seventies," added his wife, Deb. "Don't let it get you down. You had your big hit, and you don't have to prove anything."

This was not what he hoped to hear, but the lack of interest by the area's radio stations confirmed their opinions. In the end, the record got no airplay, and once again Hugh gave up on the idea of a revived music career. It wasn't meant to be, he conceded, and with reluctance continued his life far from the limelight that he had briefly enjoyed.

* * * * *

By the time Hugh's daughters reached college age, he had long given up on the idea of ever performing again. However, that would change the weekend he prepared to go on a fishing trip with two of his friends from work. For it was then he learned something that would redirect the course of his life.

"Hey, Pomp, you're a hit again," declared Bret Manning, his assistant at Cobalt HVAC.

"What are you talking about?"

"Your song has gone viral on You Tube."

"Huh? 'King Kong Katy?' Stop busting my chops."

"No. Really. You got over five hundred thousand hits. Well, not *you* exactly. This guy remixed your song. It's hysterical. Check it out."

Hugh opened his laptop and found the video. He recognized the opening bars of his song, and then was surprised when it took on a rap beat. A tattooed white kid in jeans hanging perilously on his skinny hips delivered the lyrics.

"She may be big, she may be burly, but King Kong Katy is my girly..."

"What the...?"

"I told you. Look he's got some old clips of you on it. Cool, huh? I think it's a riot. You're famous again, man. You da buzz, Cuz!"

Hugh experienced a mix of feelings. *How dare the young punk mock me?* was his first reaction, but he gradually came to see the video as a sort of homage. It wasn't as if the kid was deliberately lampooning his composition. He was adapting it to his musical style—the style of the day—and not doing an entirely bad job of it either. Hugh was no fan of rap and hip-hop, but he'd heard and seen enough of it to know what was bad and what was good.

When he returned from his fishing trip three days later, even his wife was excited about the You Tube video.

"The kids love it, honey. They say their friends really do, too. It's got more than a million hits so far, and some guy saying he's an agent called for you."

"You got to be kidding," replied Hugh, who looked at the name on the piece of paper his wife handed him.

"The man said he'd like to handle you, babe."

"Handle me? What for? Because of some goofy video? What's to handle?"

After Hugh put his fishing gear away, he went online. Sure enough, well over a million people had seen the new rap version of his only hit. After watching it several times, he began to warm to it. *Not bad,* he thought. *What the hell. At least my song has a new life. Better than being dead and forgotten.* He then dialed the number on the piece of paper, fully expecting some kook to answer.

"Mr. Fox's office," responded a woman's warm voice.

Hugh identified himself, asked for Marv Fox, and was immediately put through to him.

"Glad you returned my call, Pomp. That's what they called you, right? Your video is exploding. Nearly two million hits now. I just checked. Man, that's great!"

"I didn't even know about it until a friend told me. Not sure how the guy got permission to use my song, or if he even did."

"Who cares? He's put you back in the spotlight. I can get you some bookings. You got any new material, Pomp?"

"A few songs. Have an album I did years ago that never got played."

"How about we get you rolling again? Come by my office tomorrow. If the video keeps getting hits, there's no telling what we can do."

Hugh thought about it for a moment and then out of curiosity agreed to meet with the agent the next day.

Fox, a short balding man in a striped bowtie, greeted him enthusiastically with the news that the "King Kong Katy" video had double the hits since they had last spoken.

"Yeah, I saw that. Wish I had a dollar for everyone watching it."

"Wouldn't that be great, but I think we could make some dough here. I'll rep you for standard. That's why I called you. Since we spoke, I've done some checking. I can get you gigs at some pretty decent places. You got to do some traveling, but that's the nature of the business. You know that."

"Frankly, I put all that behind me years ago. I got a family now, so I don't want to be spending my life on the road singing for some local yokels in a Elks Hall somewhere."

"Totally understand. But hear me out, okay? There's a tour you can join called *Voices From Yesteryear*. Some good people featured, like Fabian and Gary Lewis. You know them, right? Others, too."

Hugh nodded, wondering if Fabian still had his looks, since he'd never had a voice.

"Anyway, the show is playing in New England and is going to land here in Manchester this weekend, so it's right in your own backyard. You can decide whether you want to go with it when it heads to the Midwest. Just do a few shows in this area."

"I'll think about it, but at this point I'm not really inclined, Marv."

"Well, mull it over, Pomp. Call me no later than Wednesday. I think this could jumpstart your career."

"Nothing to jumpstart. The engine has been cold for twenty years," replied Hugh, turning to leave.

"Oh, I almost forgot. I contacted Faux Records in Boston. They said they'd like to do a session with you and maybe lay some tracks."

"Really? When?"

"Up to you . . . sooner the better, though. When you available?"

"I'm ready now," answered Hugh, suddenly enthused by the prospect of returning to the recording studio.

"Hold on. Let me buzz them."

Hugh took a seat while Fox made a call.

"Hey, I got the original 'King Kong Katy' guy here. He wants to record right away. Huh? Tomorrow?" Fox looked at Hugh for confirmation. "Yeah, that works. See you at 10."

* * * * *

When Hugh told his wife about the recording session, she was enthusiastic but expressed reservations.

"Don't expect too much, hon. Remember how disappointed you were when your last album didn't go anywhere. It was a gloomy time for us. You know how tough the music business is. You were on top once. Isn't that enough?"

"Hey, I'm just going along with it, but you never know when something hits. I think I got some decent tunes. If they get some airplay . . . Look, don't worry. I've been there before, so I have no giant expectations. Let's see what happens, okay?"

"Hey, you *da Pomp*," said Deb, smiling and putting her arms around Hugh.

"Darn right. The *Pomp* lives!"

Hugh managed to record several of his songs in the six hours he had at Faux Records. The crew at the studio was very workmanlike and showed little emotion during the session. On the other hand, Fox was clearly ecstatic with the results.

"There are hits there. I can tell. I'm taking the CD to every station in the area. Starting tomorrow. Glad you're on board with the *Voices From Yesteryear* show. Just sing some of these songs, and we'll sell loads of the recording there."

Despite his reservations about taking to the stage again, in the end Hugh could not resist the opportunity to join the cast of the once-famous crooners.

"It'll be a hoot. Maybe I can do a duet with Fabian. Then everyone will see who has the better voice."

"C'mon, Kermit the Frog has a better voice than his, but he is . . . *was* pretty," quipped Deb. "From the ad, he still looks like a hunk."

"I'll introduce you to him, if you promise not to go all horny schoolgirl on me."

"Okay, but I'll probably throw my panties on stage when he's performing."

* * * * *

Hugh rehearsed his songs in the days that followed in preparation for the show Saturday night at the Armory. He accompanied himself on a small electric keyboard that he kept in the basement and would do the same on stage. When the big day arrived, he felt confident that he was back in his old form. He was told he had fifteen minutes at the start of the program before Gary Lewis appeared. He had met the singer in the seventies when "King Kong Katy" was still on the charts and had liked him. He hoped Lewis might invite him to accompany him on one of his hits, especially his favorite, "Rhythm in the Rain."

As planned, he met Fox at the auditorium a couple of hours before curtain. During that time there would be an audio check and he could loosen up his vocal cords and relax. Maybe meet his follow performers, he hoped. The stage manager directed Hugh to the dressing room, which he would share with others in the show. No one was present when he entered the cavernous room. A dozen metal folding chairs and a long table with food and soda occupied the otherwise drab space.

"Great, we can chow on the goodies they got on the table for all the acts," said Fox, eyeing the mounds of cold cuts.

"Maybe we should wait until the others get here," suggested Hugh.

"The headliners never touch this stuff. It's for the second stringers. C'mon, take advantage of the showbiz perks before the techies and crew descend."

A half hour before the show was to start, Fabian and Gary Lewis appeared. They sat apart across from Hugh and said nothing to him, despite Hugh's overtures to catch their attention.

"They're in their zones," said Fox, noticing Hugh's failed attempts to communicate with the one-time stars.

"Yeah, maybe," responded Hugh feeling snubbed.

Just before 8 PM, the stage manager informed Hugh that he was on and to get in position. Hugh stood behind the musty stage curtain and awaited his introduction. He had butterflies but knew from past experiences that they would pass as soon as he began performing.

"Ladies and Gentlemen, we start off this evening's show with the man who put the *Pomp* in Circumstance. Let's hear it for Hugh Pompeo."

Hugh was pleased with the warm reception he received and launched into his first song. But to his chagrin, it received little enthusiasm from the audience.

"Play 'King Kong Katy,'" shouted a voice from the crowd, and others followed with the same request.

Damn! Hugh thought. *They don't want anything new.* He reluctantly played the first few notes of the old song, and the crowd erupted. But when he began the vocal part he was greeted with boos. *What the hell do they want?* he wondered, feeling deep frustration. And then it occurred to him that they wanted him to play the new version that was such a hit on You Tube. *Screw that!* Hugh stopped singing and walked off the stage, carrying his portable keyboard. The disapproving sounds followed him and got louder as he climbed down the few steps to where his wife had been sitting and guided her to the auditorium's nearest exit.

"Oh, honey. I'm so sorry. It was just a bunch of dumb kids wanting the rap version like on You Tube," said Deb, trying to console her husband.

"That's it. I'm done. It was stupid of me to get back involved. I'm a one hit wonder, and I'll stay that way."

"You're the number *one* wonder to me, sweetheart."

Hugh stopped and turned to his wife and planted a long kiss on her lips.

"And that's what really counts to me, honey."

* * * * *

A month passed before Hugh heard again from Fox. He was both surprised and confused by what he was told.

"Your new song has been playing on the radio, and this week it's breaking into the Billboard Hot 100."

"What are you talking about? I haven't heard anything about it."

"Have you been listening to the radio?"

"Not really," admitted Hugh.

"Well, it's been getting airplay in Boston, New York, Chicago, and LA. Oddly enough though, not so much around here. But who cares? Manchester isn't exactly the epicenter of the music world."

"So what? It will fizzle like the last song I had on the charts. Then what?"

"Yeah, it will fizzle if you don't get out there and support it. It's a great tune, and it could go all the way. You going to let this opportunity get away from you, man?"

"I've had my shot . . . my fifteen minutes of fame. That's fine with me. More than most people get."

"Well, I'm sad you feel that way. The people at Faux Records think it's a winner, but it needs a push from you to make it that. C'mon, Pomp. You don't have to be remembered as a has-been. The Vibe in Chicago wants you there tomorrow night. It's a huge venue. You'll get a lot of print. Don't throw it away. "

"Bye, Marv," said Hugh, pressing the 'End' button on his cellphone.

"Who was that?" asked Deb, when he emerged from the basement.

"No one. Just some guy selling fantasies," answered Hugh, removing a beer from the refrigerator.

"Huh?"

"Nothing, *really*. A salesman."

* * * * *

That evening the Pompeos ordered a pizza and watched a movie On Demand. It had been years since Hugh had seen "Eddie and the Cruisers," about a rock star who vanishes after a hit album.

"It's so sad, but he had to get away to save himself," said Deb during the closing titles. "Just think what might have been though. He was really talented. All the great music the world lost."

"It wasn't real, Deb. Just a story . . . *fiction*," replied Hugh.

"Yeah, I know, *but* . . ."

Hugh lay awake most of the night reflecting on his life. At the first sign of dawn, he slipped out of bed and quickly packed some clothes. He left a note for his wife on the kitchen table and called Fox as he drove to the airport.

Poetaster

Look at the wreck that is my verse

    Awkward, flimsy, and poorly shaped

No Auden or Elliot does my pen excel

    Just words and sentences I have aped

*

I'll not pretend my lyrics are sonorous

    Each rhyme reveals an inane attempt

My couplets and quatrains dull as ever

    Never reaching the heights I've dreamt

*

He writes with a feeble hand, the critics all say

    Better off he dig a ditch

Suit him more than his arid quill

    That yields such awful kitsch

Mama's Hurts

To sympathy with hopes and fears it heeded not.
— Percy Bysshe Shelley

Mama makes a small hurt into a big one. The other day she stubbed her toe carrying the laundry basket to the clothesline and you would have thought she broke her leg. She limped around for two whole days and made grunting and whimpering noises whenever she was near Daddy and me. I didn't say much after she first told me, because I didn't want to encourage her. Daddy just ignored her like he usually does.

"All she wants is attention, for God almighty's sake," he mumbled. "Darned if I'll give it to her anymore, Jenny. She just tries to make everyone feel sorry for her."

Guess he's right. She really does make a big deal out of something, 'specially if you go along with her. And it seems the more attention you give her, the more she wants. After all these years, I know enough to say nothing much about her hurts. I mean, I'm sympathetic at first, but when she keeps moaning and groaning, I try to ignore her like Daddy does.

I guess I was 8 years old the first time I heard Daddy tell Mama she was making a mountain out of molehill. I asked him what a molehill was and he just said it's something your Mama does every time she wants people to pay attention to her. I still wasn't totally sure what he meant, but after a while I caught on. Because every time Mama got all worked up about small things that happened to her, Daddy repeated the phrase.

"Iona, you're making a mountain out of a molehill."

* * * * *

There were times when Mama seemed cured of her complaining, but then she'd start in again. And like before, everything became a huge crisis. If she got a paper cut, she'd act like she was going to bleed to death. One day she was helping me with my homework and caught her finger on my math sheet. At first I thought she was having some kind of terrible attack. Then I saw a tiny drop of blood on my assignment sheet and knew she got one of those weird scratches that feel like a razor on your skin.

"Oh, Jenny, look what happened to me! Mama really hurt herself."

She rushed to the bathroom and ran her wounded finger under water for the longest time. When she came out she showed me the cut, and I could hardly see it. She complained about it for days until nobody paid any mind to her.

Mama had a lot of little accidents and hurts that became big dramas as I got older. Once she was all worried about some lump in the back of her ear. She fussed about it for what seemed forever.

"I think it's a tumor," she kept saying over and over, until my Daddy took her to the doctor. Turned out it was some kind of oil deposit that was harmless.

"A mountain out of a molehill!" scowled Daddy.

Another time she was certain she was having a stroke because her fingertips were numb.

"I can't even tell if the dish water is hot. I know something is really wrong," she fretted night and day.

At first she refused to go to the doctor. I think it was because she knew it wasn't anything bad. But she kept talking about it, so my Daddy ordered her to have it checked out. When she finally did, she learned it was a just pinched nerve in her neck that was causing it. Nothing fatal. It went away a few days later.

"Another damn molehill, Iona!"

* * * * *

Mama's complaining seemed to get worse when I was in high school. I'd come home and be greeted with a dark report about her newest pain or mishap instead of a cheerful hello. It got so I wouldn't even respond to her gripes, and Daddy sure didn't. But that didn't stop Mama from trying to get us to show concern. Her complaint was a trap for sure, and we knew it. One word from either one of us in response to her latest misery, and we'd pay for it. She'd go on and on about how she was suffering because of this or that until we wanted to scream at her.

It got so she really drove us crazy, and Daddy wanted her to get therapy for what he called a "mental deficiency."

"Iona, you got to stop bellyaching about nothing all the time. You should go see a shrink. Because this just isn't normal behavior for a grown person."

Mama would have no part of therapy, however, and for a time after Daddy's suggestion that she get professional help, she stopped complaining a little. Then it started up again, and it was soon worse than ever. She was always saying that her stomach hurt her . . . that she was having what she claimed were "gruesome pains" in her abdomen.

"Now she's bellyaching about bellyaches," muttered Daddy warily.

However, this time Daddy did not force her to see the doctor. He was certain that it was just another of her imagined ills. Besides, Mama did not want any part of a doctor's visit, because of the criticism that always resulted when it turned out that she had nothing horrible. A mountain out of a molehill, like daddy said.

* * * * *

For several months Mama went around clutching her stomach

and mumbling that she had something terrible and that nobody cared. Finally, it got too much for us to bear, so against her will we drove her to the hospital emergency room. We couldn't get ahold of her doctor, even though we kept calling him. *Maybe he knows that Iona Billings is up to her old tricks and doesn't want to deal with her,* I mused.

The hospital kept Mama overnight for tests, and then we got the worst news you could ever imagine. Mama had terminal stomach cancer. We couldn't believe it. It just didn't seem possible, because she never had anything severe before when she complained. Maybe we should have brought her to the doctor's sooner, I told my Daddy, and he said that was silly, that we couldn't have known she was really sick.

All during the weeks that followed, Mama didn't complain once, although she was in a heap of pain. In fact, she acted like everything was just fine even though it was far from it. Daddy and me did everything we could to make her confortable. And for a while I almost forgot that Mama was really sick. On the other hand, Daddy was a wreck and kept acting like he was the one about to go over the cliff.

"Oh, I just can't believe your poor Mama is going to die. What are we going to do without her? I'm just not sure how we'll go on when she's gone. This house will go to seed fast. Neither one of us knows how to cook or do all the other things your Mama does around here. This is such a terrible disaster," whined Daddy.

Mama suddenly appeared in the kitchen where we were sitting and shuffled past us toward the sink. Halfway there, she turned and spoke in her weakened voice.

"Oh, for the love of God, Henry, stop making a mountain out of a molehill!"

A Hell of a Day in Heaven

> *It is not of some importance but is of undamental importance that justice should not only be done, but should manifestly and undoubtedly be seen to be done.*
> — Lord Hewart

While the gathering of homicide victims in the Eternal Kingdom was one of the year's most anticipated events, it was a day of mixed feelings for those who had perpetrated the crimes against them. To the multitude of offenders, a few hours away from the fires of Hell was a welcome one, but having to face their victims was irritating, if not unpleasant, to many. As serial killer Giles Blake observed, it was "the fly in the ointment."

"Would be a decent break, but facing these whiners ruins it. What do they have to complain about? They're in paradise, for Chrissakes!"

Conway Helm, Blake's fellow mass-murderer, agreed. "All we did was send them to a better world, and for that we burn. Not fair!"

"Yeah," complained another violent predator, "We should have been thanked for what we did, but instead we're sentenced to endless damnation. The world is a messed-up place. The do-gooders don't do the great thing we do. We give people what they pray for—life everlasting in Eden."

His lament was joined by those of countless other murderers, and then the moment arrived when they were transported upward. The instant the transgressors appeared before the waiting crowd, it fell silent. For a protracted moment, the criminals peered out at their victims from an elevated stage waiting for what they knew would happen next.

They were quickly paired with their former quarry and directed to a private space where what was called "The Reckoning" would take place. The wrongdoers were not permitted to speak unless asked to do so by their victims. In that event, the slayers were required to respond as succinctly as possible. No appeals for forgiveness or mercy were allowed. There could be no redemption for those consigned to the netherworld. The sole purpose of their appearance was to provide their former prey an opportunity to rebuke them for their heinous deeds. Not all victims participated in the annual ritual, but for those who chose to do so, it was often a worthwhile experience.

* * * * *

Giles Baker had been through the procedure dozens of times and had learned to turn a deaf ear to the admonitions and entreaties of his kills. He had quickly grown weary of the same old question: "Why did you do it?" *These people just didn't get it*, he'd concluded. *I didn't kill them because of what they did. They always think it was about them. I did what I did because it felt good. The pleading and begging got me off. It made me feel alive . . . the only time I ever did.*

After listening to 11 of his 17 victims, all he felt was satisfaction over what he'd done. *Moaners . . . deserved what they got.* Giles was prepared for the predictable drop back to Hades, since he figured he'd seen all of his complainants, when a small figure appeared before him.

"I grant you permission to speak," the young woman said, in a near whisper.

For a moment, Giles did not recognize her. When he did, he was surprised and agitated.

"You!" he spat.

"Yes, me," replied the woman, her voice gaining volume.

"You were my biggest disappointment. You just stood there expressionless as I pulled the trigger. Shouldn't have killed you . . . a waste of good energy. But I had no choice. You could ID me."

"I wasn't going to bother, but I thought I'd thank you."

"What?" hissed Giles, not believing what he heard. "Just let me go back down. I don't need your mocking."

"No, really, thank you. I was going to kill myself. My life was miserable. I wanted out. You saved me the trouble of committing suicide. I wouldn't have been allowed into Heaven if I had. Catholics who kill themselves are spurned and turned away."

"You're such an unfeeling bitch," growled Giles.

The woman began to laugh.

"So, you're really *my* victim."

Before Giles could respond, his body was again engulfed in flames.

Blue Zone

*Thou tyrant, tyrant Jealousy,
Thou tyrant of the mind!*
— John Dryden

Millie Flynn had been one of fourteen centenarians interviewed in Dalby, Indiana, by the U.S. Census Bureau six months earlier. The government office had been prompted to recheck its previous year's survey data because of the extraordinary number of people over 100 years old in the tiny southwestern farm community. Millie had resided there her entire life, and at 104, she had full possession of her faculties.

"Why do you suppose those government folks wanted to talk to me again?" she inquired of her eighty-two-year-old son, Harlan.

"Didn't they tell you it was because there were so many really old people in Dalby, Mama?"

"Yes, they did, but what of it. People live long in lotsa places."

"Guess not as many as they do here. "

"Just a coincidence, I'm sure. Making such a big deal out of it."

"Maybe it is a big deal, Mama? They say in the newspaper that there are more people over 100 than any other place in the country. Now that's kinda *something*."

"Coincidence is all. Next time they'll be in a dither cause nobody lived to be 50 somewhere else. Things just happen in this world."

"Well, maybe, but a bunch of reporters think it's a good story and they're starting to come here by the carloads."

"For what, to see a bunch of rickety 100 year-olds? Silly. Must be stuff more important to tell about someplace else."

"Maybe a slow news week, mama."

"Got a call this morning from this professor at the university. Asked to interview me. Told him I was busy painting the house. He was at a loss for words wondering how someone 104 years old could be doing that. Didn't laugh. Thought I was serious. Foolish man."

"Well, you did fix the cement steps last year. Remember?"

"'Course I remember. Don't forget nothing."

"I know, mama, but maybe you should talk to them fellas. Everybody else is."

"Not me. Got better things to do with the time I got left."

"What things, mama?"

"None of your business, Harlan."

"Oh, excuse me. Didn't think it was top secret."

"It ain't. It's just . . . *stuff*."

"Need help?"

"Now why would I need help?"

"Just asking, mama . . . just asking."

"Things I can do without someone standing over me waiting for me to fall."

"Okay then, I'll be back to check in on you tomorrow," said Harlan, rising slowly from the couch. "I've got your list for the store. You sure this is all you need?"

"If I needed more, I'd have it on the list."

"Fine, see you tomorrow, mama."

On his way to his car, Harlan encountered a man and a woman.

"Sir, is this the home of Millie Flynn?"

"Yes, it is. Why do you ask?"

"We're from *People Magazine*. We'd like to ask Mrs. Flynn some questions."

Well, good luck with that," said Harlan, climbing into his 15 year-old Buick LaSabre.

* * * * *

Max Calberry, owner of the Dalby Motel, calculated there were at least a dozen reporters staying at his place. The sudden burst of business pleased him and other business owners in the town that also had enjoyed a financial windfall.

"Got no rooms left. Two reservations called in just this morning. Raking it in," boasted Max to his cousin, Howell Burns, a local realtor.

"I've been getting inquiries from all over the country about houses for sale. People think we got the Fountain of Youth here in Dalby," declared Howell.

"I dunno . . . not so sure this is such a good thing," mulled Carl Lester, the town sheriff.

"Why's that?" asked Max.

"More people, more crime."

"Yeah, but more people, more money, and we could use an influx of cash in the town coffers. All kinds of work needs to be done around here," observed Howell.

"I hear you, but with fortune comes folly, they say," said Lester.

"Not always. This can be good for everybody. Property values are bound to rise. Yours too, Carl."

"We're all getting near retirement. Think of how much more we might get for our houses. Get the heck out of this climate. Move to Florida. Be able to buy cheap down there," added Max.

At this point in the conversation, Harlan entered the Keystone Cafe and joined the group of regulars.

"Hey, Harlan, we're all gonna get rich," spouted Max.

"How's that, Max?"

"By selling our piece of the Fountain of Youth."

"Huh?"

"Howey says our property is going to be worth a bundle because of all the hoopla about the town's ancient elders," offered Max. "Could sell the motel for a heap and retire in luxury where it never snows."

"Don't think anyone would get my mom to sell out."

"Well, Harlan, no disrespect intended, but how much longer is she going to be around at 104? You clearly got good genes, so when she goes to her reward, you can live high on the hog," said Howell, raising his cup of coffee to his lips.

"No disrespect taken, but I'm not high on living high on the hog. Just be happy to stay put here in Dalby and give any money from my mom's house to my grandkids. She'd like that. Already suggested it."

Howell's cellphone rang, and he excused himself from the table. In a couple minutes he returned, all smiles.

"Just sold the old Lambert place for top dollar to some retired folks in Minnesota. They're convinced that this town will assure them longevity. They said they believe there's something in the soil or water here that helps people live so long. I got to go to draw up the papers. I'm telling you guys, this is a *good* thing."

* * * * *

Within six months, 300 new people, mostly seniors, had taken up residence in what had become known in the media as "Centenarian City." Gerontologists and a host of other experts on long-life continued to probe the phenomenon but hadn't reached any conclusive results. Eventually, the prevailing consensus had it that it was a numerical fluke that so many people over 100 years of age lived in the same area. This news did not stop or even slow the progression of moving trucks that arrived daily with the possessions of new Dalbyites.

"Guess the increase in the population hasn't impacted crime levels," admitted Sheriff Lester. "Of course, seniors are not known for committing felonies."

"See, I told you, Carl, nothing but good. I can't keep up with the demand for housing," said Howell, excitedly. "I calculate every house in town has increased ten to fifteen percent in value, and it's not going to stop there."

"We're going to have major TV coverage of our One Hundred Plus Club parade," boasted Town Manager Cary Atwell.

"Where'd that title come from?" asked Harlan.

"Came up with it when we were putting together the event. Needed a name to catch everyone's attention."

"Not bad, Cary."

"We got everyone but your mother to join in, Harlan. Can't you get her to go along with it . . . for the good of the community?"

"She thinks all the stir about having so many old folks in town is silly. Doesn't want to be a part of it."

"Well, would you give it another try, Harlan? It would be good to have them altogether out there. The weather's going to be nice and warm, so the fresh air would be good for them."

"Once she's set her thoughts in one direction, she's not an easy one to convince otherwise."

"Just try, okay?"

"My grandpa's hard-headed, too. He likes all the attention, but he's dug his heels in about selling his house. Says he plans to die there," offered Max.

"That can't be long. He's the oldest of the bunch. What, one-hundred-eight, right?"

"Next month, yeah."

"Spoke with Ellen and Barry, and they say their parents think the same way. Only gonna leave their places horizontally."

"Well, they have a right. Most of them have lived in their houses forever. It's their comfort zone. Thing is, they're all doing for themselves, like my mom. Pretty amazing when you think we got 14 folk over 100 living on their own in this town."

"And that's what makes Dalby so darn unique," observed Howell. "Two of them said they want to *walk* in the parade instead of ride."

* * * * *

As predicted, the day of the parade was bright and warm. Several floats decorated by high school students and staff and local civic groups gathered in the sports field just off the main street. The town's celebrated ancients were divided among the floats, with Wilbur Cowell and Harry Cosgrove taking their place at the front of the procession to walk the length of the parade route. Precisely at noon, the cavalcade got underway. It ended four blocks away in the parking lot of the Elk's Club, where a tribute was to take place.

As expected, several members of the media were in attendance with their microphones and cameras.

"Welcome, my fellow Dalbyites, future residents, and visitors to what has become known worldwide as 'Centenarian City' because of these remarkable people here before you," proclaimed Atwell.

"It would have been perfect if your mom had joined in," whispered Howell into Harlan's ear.

"Sorry," said Millie Flynn's octogenarian son. "Said she'd rather be in her garden than on display here like some kind of oddity."

"Mabel Calloway, who herself will turn 100 next year, has made one of her famous cakes for members of our One Hundred Plus Club," continued Atwell.

On cue, with the help of two assistants, 99 year-old Mabel wheeled out a cart containing her confectionery handiwork. The Town Manager then sliced the cake for the honorees, putting aside the last slice for the absent Millie Harlan, which inadvertently fell to the ground and consequently was deposited in a waste barrel. The esteemed elders ate their cake with zest and received loud cheers from the audience for doing so.

"So, the real secret of great longevity is *cake*," joked Atwell.

Following the event, the prized centenarians were escorted out of the hall and returned to their respective homes where they all took their routine afternoon naps. By evening, however, news quickly spread that none of the elders had awakened. All 13 had apparently died in their sleep.

Shocked and baffled by the tragedy, the townspeople were further aghast when the coroner announced the deceased had been poisoned.

"Arsenic," declared Dr. Donald Jason at an impromptu news conference.

"How?" shouted reporters.

"Cake," replied the coroner. "Mabel's cake was loaded with it."

* * * * *

An hour earlier, Sheriff Lester had been at the alleged murderer's bedside. Next to him stood the woman's elderly daughter.

"She's got late-stage cancer. I was totally amazed that she was able to make that cake and give it out. It was something she really wanted to do," said Clair Calloway, unaware of why the sheriff was visiting her mother.

Lester bent to within inches of the dying woman's ear and whispered to her. "Why'd you do it, Mabel?"

"Knew I wouldn't make it to 100 and hated them for beating me to it. Now who's the oldest in Dalby?" said the former baker with a faint cackle.

When Harlan reported the calamity to his mother, she replied, "Hope this town learned that you can't have your cake and eat it too."

Despite the deep sadness he felt for what had happened, Harlan could not keep from smiling.

Christopher Lee's Eyes

Tis the eye of childhood that fears a painted devil.
— Shakespeare

Sandra Cotton was abruptly awakened by the shrieks of her eight-year-old son. She leapt from bed and ran to his room where she found him sitting up and trembling.

"What's the matter, honey?" she asked, wrapping her arms around him. "My God, you're so hot . . . sweaty. Let me get a towel to dry you off."

"Don't leave, Mommy!" squealed Darrell.

"Why are you so scared, sweetheart."

"I'm afraid of . . ."
"Of what, Darrell?"
"The man with the red eyes."
"Red eyes?"
"In the movie Daddy took me to."
"Huh? What did he take you to see?"
"A man bit girls, and they screamed."
"Oh no, he took you to *that* movie. He shouldn't have."
"Then there was blood on his long teeth."
"It wasn't real, dear. Just silly make believe."
"I saw his red eyes in the dark. Over there," pointed Darrell, in the direction of his closet.

"Look," assured Sandra, pointing to where her son had, "See .

..there's nothing there. You were just having a bad dream. Go back to sleep, sweetie. I'll leave the light on, okay."

"Can you stay with me, Mommy?"

"No, honey. Mommy's got to get some sleep for work tomorrow, and you'll be fine. There's nothing to be scared about."

Despite her son's pleadings, Sandra returned to her bedroom and climbed into bed, elbowing her sleeping husband.

"Wha . . . why?"

"You took Darrell to see 'Horror of Dracula?' I told you not to. He's too young for that kind of movie."

"He wanted to go. It wasn't *that* bad."

"Oh yeah? Well, he was just screaming about a man with red eyes."

"Christopher Lee."

"Huh?"

"He was Dracula."

"Great . . . *just* great! Well, the next time he wakes up screaming, you go to him."

"No problem."

Doug Cotton was fast asleep when his wife elbowed him again.

"It's Darrell! He's shouting for us again . . . *go!*"

* * * * *

And this was only the beginning. The *man with the red eyes* haunted Darrell throughout his childhood. The image was indelibly etched on his inchoate mind. It was not until he reached high school that a full month went by without his thinking of the bloody sclera of what his mother had assured him was just an actor in makeup. He had wondered how the color of the white part of the eyes could be changed without hurting them.

Eventually, like most childhood nightmares, the one that had tormented him slowly faded. It was not until he was middle-aged that he again encountered the performer whose "made-up" eyes had so troubled him. It was during a close-up of a character in the film version of "Lord of the Rings" that he realized it was the same actor. Although his eyes no longer exhibited the veiny red webs that had caused Darrell so many sleepless nights, he knew Lee had played the blood-lusting bogeyman from the 1958 movie his father had thoughtlessly exposed him to.

Although the now aged actor portrayed a benign figure in the later movie, Darrell could not see him as anything other than the fiend that had plagued his youth. What further distressed him was the realization that he and the actor now bore a striking resemblance to one another. Although Lee was many years older than Darrell, the two could have been close relatives, perhaps even father and son. He found this both bizarre and frightening.

Later in the week Darrell rented two earlier Lee movies. He wanted to see if the similarity between their appearances was even greater when the actor was closer to his age. Indeed, it was. They could have been brothers, even twins. This revelation sent him into a tailspin. Although he could reason that it was just an odd coincidence, there seemed something darkly portentous, even sinister, about it.

Darrell began avoiding looking into mirrors, because when he did he came face-to-face with his worst childhood fears. Occasionally, when he inadvertently caught his reflected image, he seemed almost clone of the actor.

* * * * *

Darrell's despair deepened during a casual office conversation when his colleagues were discussing what famous people they resembled. Fearing the obvious, he quietly worked his way to the back of the group. Yet even there he could not hide.

"So, who does Darrell look like?" asked Gil Foster, his best friend at the company.

"Jeez, I don't know. Maybe nobody," mumbled someone, and two other people expressed a similar sentiment.

"He does look like someone, though," added someone else.

"Oh, I know!" exclaimed another.

"Who?" Foster asked. "That guy in those dumb 'Ernest' movies?"

The remark incited a round of laughter.

"No, no! He looks like that actor in all those old Dracula movies." Darrell's heart sank, and he wanted to run from the room.

"You mean Bela Lugosi?"

"No, *not* him. What's his name? Christopher, something . . . "

"Yeah, Lee. Christopher *Lee*. Hey, you really do look like him, Darrell," said Foster.

Darrell attempted to downplay the comparison, but despite his protestations, the group quickly became more convinced that he was a dead ringer of Lee. When they called up the actor's images on the computer, it ended the debate.

"Holy crap! You sure you haven't been moonlighting in Hollywood all these years, Darrell? You could be his double."

"They call it a *doppelganger*," chimed in Patricia Harold. "Someone who is your mirror image. Hey, I'd better cover my neck around you, Darrell."

This remark hit Darrell hard, because very recently he found that he had become obsessed with the necks of younger women, and Patricia fell into that category. Every passing day he found her more appealing.

The group finally dispersed, returning to their respective offices and cubicles. Darrell was left alone with his unsettling thoughts. *I'm becoming him. Lee's character in the movie. No, that's ridiculous, but I feel something . . . an urge to . . .* thought Darrell, feeling panic set in. *Turn it off . . . all these stupid thoughts. So I look like Christopher Lee. So what? Everybody looks like someone.*

On his walk back to his apartment after work, he became horrified when he sensed he could hear the thoughts of people he passed. To his further chagrin, he also realized that he could not help but stare at virtually every young woman's neck. Each one made his heart race with a strange but profound hunger.

This is absurd. Totally freaking outrageous. You're losing it, buddy boy. Going over the edge. Stop it! Just goddamn stop it . . . please!

* * * * *

That night Darrell sat on his terrace in the chilly moonlight and observed his surroundings with greater acuity than ever before. He felt drawn to the powerful unseen forces of the primordial world. Oddly, it was a pleasant experience, despite the cold wind that pushed hard against his thin frame. An intense urge to move through the darkness of the adjoining woods to satiate a desire he could not quite define was rapidly taking hold of him.

When his doorbell rang, he knew that Patricia had arrived as planned. He opened the door and welcomed her, pressing his face into the hollow of her neck. It made his chest heave, and he quickly turned away.

"Please excuse me for a minute. I have to . . . "

Darrell disappeared into the bathroom to deal with the sudden ferocious lust he felt after contact with his pretty colleague. He clenched the sides of the sink, and then gradually lifted his head to face himself in the mirror. His eyes bled, as had Christopher Lee's in his eternal nightmare. Darrell pulled back in initial horror and repulsion, and then he began to feel himself rise off the floor and become weightless.

I'll drain her. Every sweet ounce, he thought, as his canines descended and pressed against his lower lip.

Deejay By the Numbers

Take a little time — count five and twenty.
— Charles Dickens

"One, five, ten. There! Perfect spacing."

"No. If it were zero, five, ten, it would be perfect spacing . . . *jeez!*"

"C'mon, boss!"

"Can't let you off the hook that easy."

"God, man, . . . give me a break. One, five, ten' is close enough. Nearly perfect."

"It's either *perfect* or it *isn't*. You're off by a digit."

"Well, crap, that's nothing. Give me another chance . . . *please?*"

"Why should I? You didn't deserve the first chance for what you did."

"I know . . . *I know.* I blew the backtiming to the network feed. I'm usually fine talking up to the post. Run a tight board."

"Not tight enough."

"Look, just one more shot. I'll nail it for sure"

"Okay, three digit spacing over a hundred. *Go!*"

"Ah, damn . . . that's *hard!* Okay . . . okay, one hundred-one, one hundred-five, one hundred-ten. Perfect spacing, right?"

"You're an idiot, but what did I expect. You're off again. Did you go to grade school?

"Look, I need my midday air shift. I'll get tighter."

"You're doing midnight to six until you learn to count."

"The graveyard shift? I can't be on-the-air seven hours straight, boss!"

"*Get out!*"

A Fly in the Ointment

They are other than the loud and troublesome insects of the hour.
— Edmund Burke

As cardiac surgeon Niles Bellamy was about to make an incision into his patient's left ventricle, a fly buzzed by his face and landed on the anesthetized man's mitral valve. Dr. Bellamy's knee-jerk reaction was to shoo away the insect. As he did, the scalpel in his right hand inadvertently severed his patient's atrium and pulmonary veins. Attempts were made to save the patient, but he had quickly succumbed to the doctor's terrible mistake. But as no one in the operating room had apparently seen Bellamy slice into the patient's heart, the surgeon acted as if the death was an unfortunate but natural turn of events. It was not uncommon for people undergoing such delicate surgery to die during the procedure.

"Let's close him up. Ring the morgue. Sorry people, Mr. Jennings was beyond our powers, I'm afraid," said the surgeon, quickly exiting the operating room. *Fucking fly! How the hell did it get in here?* wondered Bellamy, as he removed his blood-covered latex gloves and blockade gown.

For the balance of the day as well as the week that followed, the doctor was full of self-recrimination. He was glad he had the next few days off but unhappy that his wife was out of town on business. He desperately needed her presence to help him get through the upheaval he was in. *Jesus, I killed the guy. He probably would have been fine. Do no harm, right? Well, you sure as hell did harm, Dr. Bellamy.*

When Madeline Bellamy returned from her trip to the West Coast at the end of the week, her husband was feeling a little better. *Shit happens in the operating room*, he kept telling himself in an attempt to mitigate his sense of culpability. *Every day patients die under the knife for all sorts of reasons.* Yet, he had to fight hard to keep from lapsing back into his sense of guilt. *Why was that fly in there? There are never supposed to be insects in the operating room! It wasn't my imagination. I'm sure it wasn't. I know what I saw. That's why I tried to flick it away. Oh God, how stupid was that? You killed a man shooing away a fucking fly. What if someone had seen you do that? You'd be done as a surgeon. Maybe you should be. You let a fly break your concentration and it resulted in the death of the person you were to save. Yeah, maybe you should really be doing something else.*

Though the idea of returning to work disturbed Bellamy, a slew of commitments forced him back to the hospital—and the operating theater. As a consequence of his absence, he had four difficult surgeries to perform on his first day back. *Gird your loins and get back in the saddle, Niles. For Christ's sake, this is your life. It was an unfortunate accident. They happen, man. It wasn't deliberate. Stop persecuting yourself!*

By the time Bellamy prepped for the first operation, his confidence had mostly returned. *Just another transmyocardial revascularization. How many of those have you done? Dozens without a complication, right? So get it done, Niles. Life goes on. This is what you do, and you're goddamn good at it.*

His first procedure went smoothly, but halfway through his second, things took a disastrous turn when he saw a fly climb from the small incision he had made in his patient's chest. *Oh Jesus, What the . . .* But this time rather than swipe at it as he'd done before, he pressed his scalpel against the insect, cutting it in half. Yet with the same motion, he pushed it back into the incision's opening, severing vital tissue and causing his patient extreme hemorrhaging.

It took Bellamy a few crucial seconds to realize what he had done and then he desperately attempted to stem the effusive bleeding. His patient quickly flatlined and was declared dead shortly after. Remarkably, once again, no one in the operating room had witnessed Bellamy's actions, and as before he made no effort to assume blame. However, he was deeply shaken and cancelled the rest of his surgeries for the day. *Was it really there? Am I seeing things? How could this be happening? You killed another patient. I can't operate any more. I'm done. Totally frigging done,* he thought, changing into his street clothes.

* * * * *

That night, Bellamy contacted the head of the hospital's surgical department and informed him that he was taking a leave of absence.

"Is this because of the recent loss of your patients, Niles?"

"I just need some time, Ted. I haven't taken a breather in four years, and I need to get away for a while."

"Don't torment yourself about what happened. You know you did everything you could. It comes with the territory. You can't save everybody. That's not the way it works, Niles."

"Well, it's just gotten to me. I need to clear my head and calm my nerves. My hands are . . . I'll take a month and then be back at it."

"Do what you have to do, Niles. I understand."

"Hey, Ted, can you have maintenance check the surgical suites to make sure that nothing is getting in them? That they're totally sealed?"

"What would be getting in there?"

"Oh, I don't know. I think I saw something flying around in OR-2."

"Really? Jeez, I don't see how that's possible, but I'll have it checked out."

"Thanks, Ted. Just a precaution."

* * * * *

Bellamy pleaded with his wife, Madeline, to take a couple weeks off from her law firm, but she claimed it was impossible given the heavy caseload she had. In turn, she encouraged him to go away alone, arguing that it would be better for him to be by himself.

"You need to regain your focus and confidence . . . get some real rest, Niles. I don't know what's bugging you, but you haven't been yourself for a while."

Bugging me . . . *yeah, that's the right word. I'm going nuts because of a freaking bug,* thought Bellamy, still trying to convince his wife to accompany him.

"I just can't. These cases are crucial to the firm, and there's no one there able to take over for me. I've been working on these lawsuits for months. I'm sorry, honey. You go, and if I can get a couple of days between court appearances, I'll join you. God knows I could use a little R&R, too."

"Fine . . . fine. I'll go, but only for a week if you're not coming," pouted Bellamy.

"No, you need more than a week to return to your old self. Book three weeks, and I'll promise to come down for a few days, or at least two."

Bellamy reluctantly agreed to Madeline's plan, and the next afternoon he was on a plane headed to the Caribbean. As soon as he exited the airport terminal at his destination, he felt better. The sunshine seemed wonderful after the long grey months of winter in Cleveland. *It is good to get away. I've got to put it back together, or I won't be worth anything to anyone,* thought Niles, catching a cab to his hotel.

* * * * *

The first thing Bellamy did when he arrived at his room was to change into his shorts and take a seat on the terrace overlooking the hotel pool and nearby beach. *Yes, this is good . . . really good.* He soon nodded off as the warm sea breeze wafted over him. When he woke up an hour later, he felt even better than he had. Hungry, he called room service and ordered a sandwich and garden salad.

"Oh, and I'd like a Tanqueray martini extra dry with olives and rocks on the side."

Room service soon arrived with his order and placed it on a small table on the terrace. It was at that moment that, to his dread, Bellamy noticed a large fly near the server's head. He instantly swung at the insect and in the process struck the head of the diminutive hotel employee with considerable force. The blow caused the man to lose his balance and topple off the sixth floor balcony.

Bellamy screamed in horror as the server struck the cement skirt surrounding the hotel pool. Several sunbathers ran for cover as the pool water began to turn crimson from the runoff of the victim's blood. Vacationers on an adjacent balcony called for help as Niles remained too shocked to move. In minutes, police were pounding on his door. As soon as he responded, he was cuffed and taken to the local jail.

Witnesses at the hotel claimed they had seen Bellamy attack the hotel employee. Despite his representation by one of the best lawyers chosen by his wife, the court convicted him of murder, and he was sentenced to 20 years in the island prison.

"It was an accident. I was just trying to kill goddamn a fly," mumbled Niles repeatedly as he was led away to begin his long incarceration.

At first the prison guards joked about the behavior of their new inmate, who swatted frantically at the empty air in his small cell.

"Loco," they laughed, "El medico es un loco."

But they soon tired of the bizarre scene and began to pay little attention to the once prominent heart surgeon.

The only way Bellamy could escape the constant assault of the hundreds of flies that occupied his cell was through sleep. And even then he could often feel them land on his skin.

Consuming Dream

The universe is so vast and so ageless that the life of one man can only be justified by the measure of his sacrifice.
— V.A. Rosewarne

There was nothing Erik Lyman loved more in the world than animals, especially wild ones. He adored nature shows on television, and when he could afford it, he would go on wildlife tours and hike remote trails to catch sight of animals in their natural setting. As a youngster, he dreamed of becoming a veterinarian. This had principally been inspired by a traumatic incident in which he had witnessed a deer being struck by a car. He was only seven and the image was seared into his mind. He pleaded with his father to goto the animal's rescue, but he was told that it was too dangerous to stop and that the deer was beyond help anyway. It pained him deeply to watch the sight of the injured animal recede in the car window without being able to do something.

Lacking the necessary funds to attend vet's school, Erik went to a local community college and eventually settled for a job managing a petting zoo at the local park in the small city where he lived. From the start, he enjoyed being around the small creatures but hated the idea that they were kept in captivity. On more than one occasion he entertained the idea of setting them all free, but he knew they would likely encounter dangers on the busy streets that surrounded their habitat.

Five years into his job, at the age of twenty-four, Erik began to experience inexplicable weakness and tingling sensations in his limbs that made it difficult to get through his workday. After two weeks of discomfort, his mother pressed him to see the family doctor.

"It's probably nothing, but go, Erik . . . *please*. You never know. Maybe you have an infection from being around all those animals. They're not the cleanest things, you know. Dr. Fields can give you a prescription for it."

"I know. I have to. I've been putting it off, because I'm worried that he'll find something . . . bad," replied Erik, who had a history of hypochondria.

"For heaven's sake, Erik, every time you have a little pain it's not the end of the world. But go so your mother doesn't worry and drive *me* nuts," grumbled his father.

With his usual sense of doom, Erik made a doctor's appointment. He was soon examined and put through a series of tests. A week passed and then he was asked to return for a consultation. This made him more anxious, and no words of reassurance came from his father.

"Jeez, they don't ask you back unless there's something wrong."

The statement prompted Erik's mother to cry and his apprehension to soar.

"I'm not going back," responded Erik, defiantly.

"No, honey. You have to. Whatever it is, Dr. Fields will take care of it. He's kept you healthy since you were a baby. If you don't go, I'll go myself and find out what he has to say."

Erik finally relented and appeared for his second appointment. By then he was convinced he had a major affliction. This time his instincts proved accurate.

"Your tests revealed a potential problem, but I'm not prepared to commit to a diagnosis until we run the same test again," announced Dr. Fields from behind his desk.

"But, what do you think I have?" inquired Erik, wringing his sweaty hands.

"Until I have the results back on the repeat test, I'm not going to say. It would be premature. No sense discussing it at this stage. It's possible the first test gave a false reading. That is often the case with this particular . . .. I don't want to worry you needlessly, Erik."

"I'm already worried, Doc."

"I'll speed up the process. Probably have the results back by Thursday. Look, I'll see you then, Erik."

When Erik was back in Dr. Fields' office for his third visit, he was feeling a good deal more optimistic about his condition. The tingling in his legs had stopped and he felt like his old self. However, his improved mood was quickly dashed by the serious expression on his doctor's face.

"Hello, Erik. Well, we've got the results back, and they've confirmed the first report. It appears you have Guillain-Barre' syndrome."

"Huh? What's that?" asked Erik, his heart pounding.

"It's a disorder of the body's immune system."

"That's what made me feel weird? But I don't anymore. I feel fine now," protested Erik.

"Sorry, but it's . . . it's what you have."

"So what does this mean? Do you give me some medicine so it doesn't come back?"

"There are things we can try, but it's not a simple malady to treat, and it could get worse. You could eventually suffer paralysis.

"Can it be fatal?" asked Erik, about to wail in fear.

"Only in rare instances."

"So, I might die?"

Erik began to feel light-headed and had trouble catching his breath. All he wanted to do was get away, and he acted on that impulse, running from the doctor's office to his parked car.

Oh, my God! I'm dying . . . I'm dying, he thought as he sped home.

When he informed his parents about his diagnosis, they demanded to meet with Dr. Fields.

"No, I'm never going back there! I'm leaving . . . everything. Quitting the zoo. Going away. Not going die or be paralyzed here."

"You're not going to die, honey. Why do you say that?" responded Mrs. Lyman, gulping back tears.

"Because Dr. Fields said I might," replied Erik, petulantly.

"Calm done, son. He can treat you and get you back to good health. You're young and strong. You can fight this. Shoot, you'll be fine," offered Mr. Lyman.

That evening Erik conceived of a plan in the face of his greatest calamity. He would free all the animals at the petting zoo and go to Africa to see wild creatures in their natural habitat. It was his lifelong dream, and he wasn't going to die or become incapacitated before fulfilling it.

* * * * *

Erik went online to purchase a ticket to Tanzania. It was there in the Ngorongoro Crater that he knew he would encounter the greatest concentration of wild animals that could be seen anywhere. He knew this from watching countless documentaries on Animal Planet, his favorite cable channel. He then rented a truck for the following evening when he planned to load up the occupants of the petting zoo and release them in a vast pasture surrounded by dense woods fifteen miles away. He did not reveal his plans to his parents, and to assuage their distress, he pretended to make an appointment for them to meet with his doctor the following week.

Just before 5 PM the next day, Fred picked up the U-Haul he had reserved. He waited until it was dark to return to his place of employment to begin loading the residents of the petting zoo onto the truck. He did not have to be at the airport for his flight to Africa until 10 PM, so he figured he had plenty of time to accomplish his first goal. He had packed little for his journey, only what he felt necessary to realize his second goal—to sacrifice himself to what he loved most. If he was going to die, and it seemed a real possibility to him, he would do so in a way that protested the harsh treatment of nature's creatures. At the same time, he'd be satisfying an animal's hunger. *They can feed on me as we feed on them.* He believed it was the noblest way for his existence to end.

Removing the petting zoo animals went smoothly, but getting

them to the pasture took longer than he planned, and he had to make an end run to the airport in the rental truck rather than his car. He parked the vehicle and ran to the Swiss Air ticket counter where the attendant gave him a suspicious look when he didn't declare any baggage.

"I forwarded everything, so I could travel light," he told the skeptical airline employee, who returned his passport and license.

Erik made it through security and dashed to his departure gate just seconds before boarding ended. His flight took 19 hours, including a layover in Zurich. He spent the day in the Swiss city taking in the sights, and returned to the airport two hours before beginning the last and longest leg of his trip. He reached Dar es Salaam at daybreak and quickly found transportation to Arusha on the edge of the Serengeti in the shadow of Mt. Killimangaro. From there he took a tour bus the remaining 100 miles to Ngorongoro.

Erik reached the edge of the crater in the middle of the night. From where he settled in beneath a towering tree for the remainder of the darkness, he could hear an assortment of animal sounds, foremost among them the occasional roar of a lion and almost constant yelp of hyenas. *They do sound like they're laughing*, he thought, as sleep overtook him. When it became light, Erik dug into his backpack and removed a gray hoody and matching sweat pans and put them on. *I'll blend*, he thought. *I'll be just another creature.*

He then started down to the grassy plain that he calculated was a good 15 miles from end to end. It was dotted with animals of every species. A seemingly endless stream of wildebeests moved in single file as far as he could see. Accompanying them were countless zebras and other four-legged critters he was hard pressed to identify. *Beautiful . . . so beautiful*, he mumbled, as he continued down the steep slope.

When Erik reached the base of the crater, he surveyed his surroundings and was overcome with the magnificence of the scene before him. *It's like a dream*, he marveled, his eyes following the rapid movements of a gazelle as it was chased by a pack of hyenas. "I give myself to nature!" he proclaimed loudly, and his voice echoed across the open steppe. A profound sense of exhilaration and contentment filled him, and he galloped on all fours toward the center of the crater. *I'm here . . . I'm here for you. Come feast on me.*

Before him were two male lions, and Erik prepared himself for their attack. But they viewed him with only mild curiosity, making no move to approach him. *They're confused by my appearance*, he concluded, and continued past them. Ahead of him were several hyenas. As he closed in on them, they stood erect and ready, but they, too, made no move in his direction.

A pack of wild dogs ran by him, also paying him no mind, and a towering ostrich meandered within arm's reach of him with similar indifference to his presence. *They accept me. They see I mean them no harm . . . that I love them.* The realization moved Erik to tears, and he raised his arms toward the clear blue sky and dropped to his knees in celebration. *I am home . . . truly home.*

It was at that most sublime moment in Erik's life that he heard the crack of a rifle being fired and felt a burning sensation on the side of his head. He turned and caught the profile of a hunter in the distance. *Just a flesh wound*, he thought, climbing to his feet. It was obvious to him that he had been confused for a wild animal, and the notion filled him with immeasurable satisfaction.

In the same instant, he saw dozens of animals pursuing the hunter that had apparently shot him. He returned to a crouched position and scampered toward his protectors as they stalked the world's most dangerous predator.

"I'm with you. I'm *one* of you," Erik shouted.

At that moment, he was struck from behind by a ravenous lion and became *one* with the King of Beasts.

Turns Out

Can anything be beyond the knowledge of [things] like you?
— Pierre-Augustin

The people of Earth were excited and intrigued by the prospect of the arrival of extraterrestrials. First contact had been made a year earlier, and over the ensuing months it was clearly established that the soon-to-be visitors from Kotophostus, a planet in the Bode's Galaxy, were benevolent—indeed, exactly like the species humans had hoped they would one day encounter from outer space. Theirs was a society of peace-loving intellectuals, whose advances in the sciences, medicine, and politics far exceeded those of the human race. The aliens' historic visit held the promise of resolving many things that plagued Earth, including disease, famine, and war.

When the day finally arrived that the Kotophostusians were to arrive, all human attention was focused on their landing at California's Muroc army airfield, which boasted the world's longest runway. Traffic controllers directed the approach of the massive extraterrestrial airship. When it finally came to a stop, the visitors were directed to turn around and move their craft toward the main hangar where the vast number of dignitaries awaited.

The Kotosphostusians did not respond to the request, and traffic controllers could hear what sounded like a clamor of voice-like sounds in their headsets. After what seemed like a standoff, the spaceship took off and disappeared into the sky. Shortly thereafter, the aliens communicated with Earth.

"We did not understand what you asked."

"We wanted you to come to where our leaders were waiting to officially welcome you."

"That is what we wished as well. But we could not determine what it was you asked us to do after landing. We did not understand that directive."

"Directive? No, no. We weren't *ordering* you to do anything. We were just giving you directions to the place where we were waiting to greet you."

"Sorry, we cannot meet."

"But why? It is very important to us that we make contact. We have so much to learn from your advanced knowledge."

"Perhaps we are more advanced than you. But you asked us something that we cannot grasp. Something beyond our accumulated knowledge. Something we could not process. Indeed, an action unknown to our species."

"Would you tell us what it was we asked that you could not comprehend?"

"What is . . . *turn around*?"

Stalker 2 Stalker

Poetic Justice, with her lifted scale.
— Alexander Pope

He was everything Suzy Foxworth had dreamed of in a man—good looking, intelligent, funny, and well groomed. He was nothing like the handful of men she'd gone out with. He was certainly different. Yet she really didn't know him very well. In fact, he was only an acquaintance, if that, a classmate in an evening 19th century British literature class. She had not even talked with him, but she had witnessed his wit and cleverness in class discussions enough to know he was *the* one.

Miles Farrell sat two rows ahead of Suzy in the small amphitheater, and her vantage point enabled her to soak in his striking appearance. *Like Jake Gyllenhaal, only more handsome*, she thought. *I wish he'd notice me. I'll try to bump into him again after class.* But as before, when she was near him, she could not muster the courage to make contact. *You coward. You'll never get anywhere with him if you don't make a move. But I can't. I just can't. Wednesday . . . definitely this coming Wednesday. Just say hi, for God's sake.*

Miles was unaware that anyone in his night class had a deep crush on him. He would not have cared if he knew, since he was entirely smitten by another woman—the type he'd always fantasized being with. Unfortunately for Miles, however, she was not interested in him in the slightest. In fact, she had come to regard him as a terrible pest, and possibly a threat, because he continually hit on her, despite her obvious displeasure.

At first, Carolyn Casey was mildly flattered by his attention. She felt he wasn't bad looking, but she was dating someone else, and they were getting pretty serious. Finally, she had to deal with his unwanted advances head on.

I just need to get him off my back. He's kind of creeping me out the way he's always around and looking at me.

"I'm sorry, but I'm not interested in a relationship with you, Miles. I have a boyfriend, and we're getting engaged soon," she told him, although there were no such actual plans in her immediate future.

Carolyn had to repeat herself on several occasions, because Miles failed to heed her words.

She'll come around. Just wear her down. She won't be able to resist you forever, he thought, as he followed her home from the mall where she worked. *She's got to see that I'm right for her. We'd be so good for each other. I'm not going to settle for anything less any more. She's the one. I'm tired of the plain Jane's I've been with. No more! No more!*

Before Carolyn reached her house less than a quarter of a mile away, she spotted Miles following her and decided to have it out once and for all.

"Why are you stalking me?" she shouted, marching up to him and poking him in the chest. "I'm going to call the police and get a restraining order. What's the matter with you anyway? Haven't I told you that I'm going with someone else? What is there about *that* you don't understand?"

"I'm not *stalking* you," replied Miles, defensively. "I just like you and hoped you'd change your mind. I think we'd be cool together."

"There is no *us* together . . . ever! Are you deaf or just stupid? I'm not interested in you, so will you please leave me alone?"

"Okay . . . *okay!* I'm sorry. I just thought . . ."

Miles suddenly felt himself on the verge of tears, and Carolyn's anger was softened by his abject expression.

"Just find someone else, *please,*" pleaded Carolyn, turning and walking away.

He watched as she disappeared around the corner of her street. *Never,* thought Miles. *I'll never find someone like you. You'll see we're perfect for each other. Deep down you want me? I'll give you a few days. Then we'll see how you feel You'll change your mind.*

* * * * *

For several days leading up to Suzy's Wednesday class, she obsessed over Miles. They made love in her ceaseless fantasies, and in them he proposed to her over and over again. But as she feared when Wednesday finally arrived, she again lost her courage to approach him. It made her frustrated and depressed that the person she desperately wanted to be with remained at such a great distance because of her own timidity and lack of self-confidence.

After the class, Suzy decided to follow Miles, and it was then that she began to realize he was as infatuated with someone else as she was with him. For two days, she tracked him and found it always led to his secretly watching the same attractive young woman. *Who is she? She's prettier than me. Why doesn't he go up to her? Is he afraid she won't like him? Does he feel about her the way I feel about him? If so, we have that much in common. Whatever happens, I'm going to talk to him after class next week,* Suzy resolved.

After that Wednesday's class, however, Miles left too abruptly for Suzy in initiate her plan. Determined to finally make herself known to the man for whom she felt such unrequited passion, she followed him again. *I'll catch up to him, and finally say something . . . anything.* His route led them to the very mall where the woman of Miles's obsession worked. He took the stairs up to the third landing, and as he reached the top, Suzy summonsed the courage to call his name.

"Yeah? What do you . . . ? Oh, sorry, you're in my class at school, aren't you" he said, perplexed by her unexpected appearance.

Suzy reached the landing and for a moment was at a loss for words. Suddenly she was overwhelmed with a desire to hold him ... kiss him. "Oh, Miles!" she blurted and threw herself at him. Before they made contact, Miles recoiled and fell backwards down the cement stairs. Suzy stood frozen in shock as Miles struck his head several times and finally lay in a limp pile at the bottom. *Oh, my God! I've killed him. He's dead!*

After several moments, she entered the mall corridor and took the escalator to the main level. From there she quickly returned to her small apartment. *I can't report it. I'll go to jail. It was an accident. People won't believe I was just trying to kiss him. It will be so embarrassing. Poor Miles. Well, if I couldn't have him, no one else will now*, she thought with a growing degree of contentment. She sat alone in the dim light of her living room and then got up and made herself a snack.

When the news that Miles was found dead in the mall reached Carolyn, she felt a mixture of emotions. Foremost was a huge sense of relief. *He was stalking me again, I bet*, she thought. *Guess he got what was coming to him. He did have a nice smile though.*

Misinformation

The prophets prophesy falsely.
— Jeremiah 31

"Welcome to Judgment Day, Barry. As you've probably surmised, I'm God. Next to me here is Jesus, my son."

"I didn't think there was . . . I mean, that I'd ever be here, sir . . . ah, your Holiness. I've never been what you'd call a believer. And I never worshipped you like the priests said to."

"That worship thing has bothered me for over 2,000 years. It was never my idea, Barry. Those people down there who thought they represented me got it all wrong. Why would I want to be worshipped? What kind of a Creator do they think I am that I need human beings to venerate and adore me? Why would they think me that vain? To be thought of in that way has always disturbed me."

"Well, no offense, God, but I never did."

"No offense taken, Barry. As far as I can tell from your record, you've been a good and decent man."

"I've tried to be, sir."

"That's good enough for us, right Jesus?"

"Darn right it is!"

"Whew! Thank you, Jesus. I thought there'd be . . . well, *nothing* after death."

"You call these nothing, Barry? Here, put these wings on."

Delusions of Grandeur

There is nothing to fear but fear itself.
— Franklin D. Roosevelt

Sometimes dying quickly is the best way out. You avoid the suffering. I can't take pain, man. So I'll off myself. Bang, it's over. Best outcome for a situation like this. Load the damn gun now. Get it done, for God's sake. Stop stalling.

You have to be precise with a 22 caliber. Better shoot myself in the temple. Don't want to end up just getting injured, or become a freaking vegetable.

You've seen those jerks that didn't pay up. They got limps or disappeared permanently. You mention their names to Johnny at the bar and he just rolls his eyes like he knows something but ain't gonna say nothing.

You dumb ass, McKenna! Why'd you borrow money from a lone shark, even if you knew the guy? When it comes to dough, friendship doesn't matter to these mugs. Christ, I thought you were smarter than that. You know how it goes. Don't pay up on time with these hoods and they crush your kneecaps, or worse, they cut off your . . . no, I can't go there. I'm gonna' be sick.

Okay, so load the friggin' pistol now before you don't got a choice in the matter, moron. I could have borrowed the money from someone else . . . Uncle Cal, maybe. He was always good for it. But no, you have to borrow from a dude connected to the mob, the son of a bitchin' *mafia*. Okay . . . okay, so shut up and just do it before he gets here, you loser.

"Hey, Mac, it's me, Ace. Open up, okay. I got something for you."

Crap, he's here. Pull the trigger, you idiot. I *can't* . . . shit, I can't. I'm gutless. Screw it. Let him in to do what he needs to do. You deserve it.

"What took you so long, Mac? You hiding from somebody... or something?"

"No, Ace. I was . . ."

"Playing with yourself, I know. I brought something to give you, Mac."

"Yeah, I was expecting you. Just do it, okay? Make it fast."

"What are you talking about, man?"

"The dough I owed you last week."

"Huh? The *dough*? Oh, you mean the ten spot I lent you? Don't worry about it. Jeez, we're amigos, right?"

"You're not . . . ?"

"Here, Mac. I brought you some donuts . . . *Munchkins*."

Metatarsal Prosopagnosia

For double the vision my eyes do see.
   — William Blake

As Mark approached the urinal, he noticed that someone was in the stall next to it. *Small feet,* he thought and then wondered who belonged to them. *Must be a freshman, but, jeez, those are really tiny, about a five or six.* When Mark was about to pee, the person in the stall flushed the toilet. His curiosity overtaking him, Mark quickly zipped up his fly and went to the sink, pretending to wash his hands. He had to see who was attached to the miniature footsies.

Mark watched in the mirror as the stall door opened. To his surprise, out walked his friend, Jared, who stood a good six-feet-two-inches. Mark's immediate response was to look at his friend's shoes to verify their puny dimensions. *Why hadn't he ever noticed the deformity?*

"What?" asked Jared to the top of his friend's downturned head. "Something the matter?"

"Ah . . . yeah, man. Your feet are like a kids or girls. They should be twice that size for your height."

"What are you talking about? I wear size thirteen."

"No way. Maybe fives."

"Okay, what's the joke?"

"No joke. Look."

"Yeah, I got big feet. So what?"

"Big? Jeez, you must be blind."

"I think you're the one who's blind," said Jared, waving off his friend as he left the restroom.

Man, is he ever in denial, concluded Mark, unzipping his fly on his way back to the urinal.

When he looked down at his phallus to take aim, he let out a loud gasp.

"Where's the rest of it?"

Skin Conditions

I hate the whole race . . .
There is no believing a word they say.
　　　— The Duke of Wellington

Jerome Niarhos had no great affection for colored people. On the other hand, he had no deep animosity for them, either. He had never made a big scene about race, like his buddies in the Klan. Mostly, he didn't think it was smart for the mayor's office to be involved in the festering controversy, since a growing number of voters in Cumberland, Mississippi, now believed coloreds deserved a better fate than the one they'd gotten. Jerome was up for re-election in what had become a tight contest, and he decided to give a wide berth to what the press called the Negro Question. He'd take more of a stand when, and if, he got re-elected for what he had decided would be his last term. *Screw it*, he thought, *then I'll say what I want about all the bullshit concerning equal rights for Blacks.*

Niarhos had first been elected mayor in 1952, and he felt ten-years as a public servant was enough. He had other ambitions. It was time to make some real money, and he had settled on plans to go into business with his best friend, Fred Mullen, who owned a garage. The two would buy a Chevy franchise. Niarhos would be its business manager, and Mullen would oversee the service end. This was a solid venture from their perspective, since their only potential rival in town, a Dodge dealer, had earned a dubious reputation for overpricing repairs.

Despite the inherent aggravations in running for office yet again, Jerome felt better than he had in a long time. The dermatitis that had plagued him for years was now responding to his daily consumption of a homemade preparation of colloidal silver that his Aunt Emma had recommended. She sas the family's unofficial physician based on the nursing certificate she'd received more than fifty years earlier. While Emma had never worked in the medical field, preferring life as a fulltime housewife, she had tried her best to keep up with the recent developments in treatments for the maladies that affected her family and friends.

"You take a good gulp of this concoction twice a day and apply it to your rough spots, like those on your chin and neck, and you'll get better."

"Thank you, Aunt Emma," responded Jerome, a bit dubious given the curious nature of the solution he was given.

Despite his reservations, his aunt's record for curing family ills was legendary, so he did as she ordered, and sure enough after a few weeks, her remedy was showing encouraging results. His blemishes had cleared, as had the irritation that accompanied them. Things were definitely looking up for him, and his improved mood was becoming an asset at voter rallies. Niarhos had never been a great speaker, and because he'd been so distracted by his acute skin condition, his oratorical skills had deteriorated. In great part it was his lackluster performances at political gatherings that had allowed his opponent to gain so significantly on him. But now his renewed energy and enthusiasm was clearly having a positive effect. He was certain that in the few weeks remaining of the campaign he would forge ahead to yet another victory.

* * * * *

About the only thing that continued to weigh on Jerome's mind, however, was the growing number of disturbances caused by the protests of black people in his community and throughout the Deep South. And now to compound the problem was the news that his town was on the route of the Freedom Riders buses coming from northern cities.

"Them goddamn civil rights people from up north are coming down here to Cumberland to stir up the coloreds," grumbled Sheriff Bo "Hammy" Hamilton at the special town meeting to consider strategies for dealing with the intrusion. "I say we kick their ass when they get off the bus."

Cheers of agreement followed his suggestion.

Niarhos spoke up. "That will only make matters worse. It would be better to let them have their protest and move on. We attack them and they'll take up camp here. Then we got a heap of trouble on our hands," he reasoned.

"Nah . . . Hammy's right! We just drive them the hell out of Cumberland with fists and bats. They ain't gonna hang round here when they be gettin' their natty heads bashed in," offered Mel Carter, local leader of the KKK.

"Look, you know I'm no fan of all this race rights crap, but why draw attention to it?" responded Nairhos "That's what they want. It's the reason they're driving all around on them damn buses. Just want to agitate people and get on the news."

"So you just want to let 'em come into town and take over like they're as good as white folks? All the darkies here gonna get the same notion, and that will cause real butt aches for all of us."

"I'm just saying we got to out think these outsiders, Mel."

"Jerome's got a point there," chimed in Beverly Adams, manager of the local Winn Dixie outlet. "Why play into their hands. Best to ignore them protesters. Act like they don't matter none. If they don't get the attention they want, they'll just move on to the next town to see if they can get it there."

"We do that and we gonna look like we agree with all the shit they doin'," declared Hamilton. "Maybe a little fire on one of them buses might get 'em goin' faster."

The meeting continued past midnight without any resolution, and Niarhos called for adjournment, suggesting another gathering a few days hence.

In the black section of Cumberland, another meeting had also been held on the same subject. A plan to support the Freedom Riders had been reached quickly.

"We can't do much, but we can be there when they come, sisters and brothers" declared Reverend Wilbur Howard.

* * * * *

Less than a week before the civil rights contingent was scheduled to arrive, Niarhos had the shock of his life. As he looked into the bathroom mirror, he discovered a freakish face starring back at him.

"What the . . .!" he yelped, leaping backwards.

He slowly peeked back into the mirror and let out a deep moan. The vision that appeared before him filled him with dread.

"It can't be," he muttered, running his hands across the dark blue color of his face. To his growing dismay, he noticed the discoloration was not confined only to his head but ran down the length of his body.

In a panic, he called his Aunt Emma to report the situation.

"Afraid I just found out that that stuff I gave you to drink can cause the skin to turn color. Called Argyria. But don't fret. The article said it'll fade. Better stop drinking what I give you, hon. Best not put it on your skin neither."

"How long will it take?"

"Might be a while. Maybe a few months. Could get darker before it gets lighter, too."

Too distraught to continue talking with his Aunt, Niarhos hung up and began to scrub his face until it felt raw. Despite his efforts, the blue pigment seemed to take on an even deeper tint. When he arrived at the town hall, those people he encountered thought he was playing an odd joke on them.

"Jesus, Mr. Mayor!" exclaimed the town hall janitor. "Ya look like some kind of Martian. Scared the hooey-gooey outa me. Ain't Halloween yet, you know."

The reaction of Jerome's secretary was even more dramatic.

When he entered his office, she let out a scream and dropped her coffee cup.

"Hold on, Millie! It's just me. Got up this morning and looked like this. Aunt Emma's concoction for my dermatitis turned me blue. Says it will go away eventually."

"My lord, Jerome. I never saw anything like that. You almost look..."

"What?"

"Like a bluish toned colored man," responded Millie, hesitantly. "Your features and the dark skin..."

"So you're saying I look like an alien Negro?" responded Niarhos, making a feeble attempt at levity.

"No... I'm sorry. Didn't mean to make you feel bad. Must feel bad enough looking like that," said Millie, blotting the spilled coffee from the papers on her desk.

"It'll go away," assured Niarhos.

An hour later, he attended the scheduled meeting on the Freedom Riders dilemma. When he entered auditorium, he was met with loud laughter and snickers.

"I know I look pretty weird. The medicine I've been taking to treat my skin did this."

"Mr. Mayor, you look like you come from another planet," hollered someone in the audience.

"Or from Colored Town," bellowed another. "Say them coons sing the blues a lot, and you sure got the blues."

The comments inspired a round of laughter louder than the first.

"Okay, let's direct our attention to the matter at hand. Order! Order!" shouted Niarhos until the uproar eventually ran its course. "Thank you. We're here to continue our discussion about how to deal with the Freedom Riders, and it's still my opinion that we should ignore them rather than make a big deal about it. That's what they want, so let's not play their game."

"That's a gutless way to deal with them Yankee agitators," responded Mel Carter. "'Sides, I don't think someone the way you look right now should be telling us how we should treat them spooks."

"What do you mean, 'the way *I* look?'"

"You look more like a darkie than a white person. Don't think you should be dealing with this no more. Least not until you turn to normal color," added Hamilton.

"I'm the mayor of this town, and it's up to me to represent it at moments like this."

"You more colored than white now. So how you gonna do that?" inquired a member of the audience.

"Yeah!" agreed several others.

"We got them goddamn Freedom Riders coming here. How's it gonna look with you that way representing the town?" growled Carter.

"What's the matter with you folks. Just because I have a little skin problem you think I'm no longer qualified to do my job as mayor?"

"We can't have you standing out there looking like you do. Be embarrassing with all the press there," declared Billy Rider, the town undertaker.

"Looking like I do? What do you mean? I look like *me*, Jerome Niarhos."

"No, you don't. We didn't elect no colored as mayor," countered Hamilton.

"But, I'm *not* colored! I'm *blue* from the medicine. It's a reaction called *Argy*-something. I ain't black, for God's sake."

"Well, you sure not white."

"To hell with all of you. You're a bunch of . . . *bigots!*"

For the first time in his life, Jerome slowly began to appreciate the plight of those with different pigmentation.

"Just get out of here until you get your right color back. If you ever do," blurted Carter.

"I'm a human being with a medical problem!" proclaimed Jerome, who then stomped off the stage.

"You ain't no human with that color skin," called Carter after him.

* * * * *

Niarhos was not seen or heard from for the next two days, and then the Freedom Buses arrived in Cumberland. They were greeted by sheet-clad Klan members, town officials, and over a hundred local residents. Kept at a distance were several dozen people of color. As the large vehicles pulled up to the town square, they were greeted with chants of "Segregation Forever!"

When the buses came to a stop, the mob fell silent, anticipating the doors to open and the unwelcome passengers to alight.

When the first Freedom Rider appeared, the crowd let out a resounding gasp. Standing before them was their missing mayor holding a placard reading:

I AM
A
MAN!

My Anxiety Journal

Remembering mine affliction and my misery, the wormwood and the gall.
— Lamentations 3:19

After a series of frightening anxiety attacks, I began keeping a journal account of them when I was in my mid-thirties. I'm not really sure why I did. It might be because they represented some of the most upsetting experiences of my life. Recording these attacks required that I think back several years to recall the first few. However, these harrowing encounters had been so seared into my mind that it was easy to remember them in detail. What I catalog below are those occurrences that stand out most in my mind. Of course, for every one of these, there were dozens of a lesser nature.

Circa 1965: This was the first time I was hit by what I came to call Panic Bombs. I was ten years old, and I truly thought I was dying. I had no idea what was happening to me. My heart pounded, I couldn't catch my breath, and I was sweating so much that my pajama top was soaked through. My father thought I was just acting up—that is, being overly dramatic (which, in fairness, I did have a tendency to be)—but he soon sensed that I was going through something unusual. He tried to assure me that I would be okay, despite my breathless pleadings to get me help. Not having a family doctor, he took me to the emergency room of the nearby hospital.

By the time we arrived, my feeling of doom had substantially diminished. By the time the ER physician examined me, and found nothing wrong, I felt okay.

"You say his heart was beating fast and he was perspiring, Mr. Coven?" asked the young medico.

"Yeah, he looked like he was going to bounce of the walls. Had me all confused about what to do. Figured coming here was the smart thing to do," replied my father, eyeing me warily.

"It's always good to seek medical attention when things like this happen, because you never know. But as far as I can tell he really is fine. Can't see anything out of the ordinary. Sometimes kids display symptoms that scare parents but really mean nothing. The growing body can behave strangely at times. If he has another episode, bring him back, and we'll run some tests. But, I doubt you'll have to return." He was right—we didn't.

April 1973: My second encounter with what I think Mark Twain called the "screaming fantods"—struck me when I was nearly nineteen. By then I was in the army and on my way to Vietnam. I know you're thinking that the prospect of going into a war zone would cause anybody anxiety, but I'm not sure that was true in my case. This was the first panic attack I had as an adult (or nearly an adult), and it felt far more intense than the one I had eight years earlier. Anyway, I was working as the company clerk (just like Radar O'Reilly on TV's *M.A.S.H.*), and as I was typing the Morning Report, I began to have major heart palpitations. I left the orderly room and stood outside as the bump-de-bump-bump worsened. It had to be a heart attack, I thought, and started heading toward the base's sickbay near the mess hall. Every step was torture, because I thought I was about to keel over dead. Well, similar to my first Panic Bomb, my normal heartbeat returned as the medic was about to take my pulse.

"You seem okay to me, corporal," said Spec. 5 Holmes. "Maybe you ate something that didn't agree with you. Of course, that could be anything from an Army mess hall, right? At least, you don't have the GIs."

The episode really shook me up, and for the rest of the day, I expected the heart palpitations to return. Thankfully, they didn't. Not for another four years.

December 1977: At a Christmas party with my girlfriend, I rode out my next anxiety attack in a bathroom. I kept praying it would pass and that I would not die. I stood looking at myself in the mirror as my body trembled and beads of sweat rolled down my face. I was holding the metal towel rack so tightly that my fingers began to bleed. The sight of the blood compounded my horror. I could hear myself whimpering like a child, and then tears began flowing from my eyes. This was it, I thought, as I began to pound the wall with my fist. The noise drew the attention of the party's host, who asked if something was wrong through the bathroom door. It took what little was in me to speak and assure her that, yes, everything was fine. I told her I was just getting something off the bottom of my shoe. Doubt she believed it, but strangely—and thankfully—the exchange had the effect of bringing me around. I was able to rejoin the gathering, although I still felt shaky for the rest of the evening. My girlfriend noticed that I wasn't myself. I told her I had an upset stomach, which wasn't far from the truth. After my anxiety attacks, I always felt a little nauseous and was certainly drained.

Spring 1979: At the Pieces of Eight Bar in Houston, I ordered a gin and tonic and then the bottom dropped out. A Panic Bomb struck me, and the Day-Glo walls of the disco lounge closed in on me. I gulped for air and lost my balance, toppling from my barstool. When I staggered to my feet, the bartender gave me a disgusted look. He said I'd had too much, and he wouldn't serve me any more. I didn't care because all I could think about was getting away from there. I had to navigate the crowded dance floor to do so. In the process, gyrating bodies battered me. On my way to the exit, I started to feel dizzy again and found myself grabbing the arm of an attractive young woman for balance. She saw that I was in trouble, and instead of pushing me away, she escorted me to the door. By then, I was sweating profusely and my body was seized by tremors. I stumbled to the parking lot without thanking my Good Samaritan. By the time I reached my car, my heart had literally stopped beating. At least, I believed it had. I crawled into the back seat and remained there immobilized and moaning. Eventually, after perhaps 20 minutes, the storm passed, and I found the strength to drive home.

Summer 1979: My therapist has tried to get at the root of the problem, but I don't think we've made much progress. I'm still in the dark about the cause of my attacks. Something in my DNA, concluded the shrink, after I can't recall any childhood traumas before my first Panic Bomb attack. She prescribed tranquillizers, but the idea of taking meds for the attacks turns me off. I try to get my emotions under control without using them. That's how we are in my family. I recite my mother's favorite lines from the poem *Invictus:* "I am the master of my fate. I am the captain of my soul." After a while, I think I'm gaining ground on my mystery affliction. Still, I believe it is only a matter of time until I let my guard down, and then bam . . . another bomb blast to my senses. I'm aware that just thinking about it makes me vulnerable to attack, so I try to build an insurmountable wall to keep the devil at bay. I wonder if I will always have to live with this.

Spring 1981: I was driving down the highway with a friend when I suddenly felt my body go cold. The demon is out of its hiding place, I thought, and I was right. My heart was playing hopscotch, and I felt like I was about to crap my pants. My hands were leaving trails of perspiration on the steering wheel. The oxygen was gone—or so it seemed—and I gulped frantically. I was certain I was suffocating. I thought of the Valium I carried and cursed myself for not taking it. But I wouldn't take a prescription drug. Not for stupid emotional eruptions. Maybe cancer. *I am the master of my fate,* I reminded myself. But I still felt like I was jumping out of my skin. As soon as we got to the next exit, I took it. My buddy asked me what was up, and I managed to say that I had to take a piss. Thank God there was a McDonalds ahead, but as quickly as the Panic Bomb came upon me, it left. I went to the restroom and doused my face in cold water. *Fuck! Fuck! Fuck!* I muttered pathetically, as I dried my face.

October 1983: My wife and I were in our local Safeway doing the week's grocery shopping. We were at the checkout register, and I noticed the cashier had a face like an animal. When I looked around, I was startled to find that all the customers had taken on features similar to hers—long ears, pig-like snouts, and furry cheeks. I then noticed my breathing was impaired and my heart was rattling in my chest. I had to get outside, I told my wife and then dashed for the door. She called after me, but I just waved and continued on. During the ride home, she asked me what had happened, and I told her that people in the market stopped looking human to me. She asked me what I meant, and I told her that I was probably having a migraine headache, although I'd never had one. She said nothing more for the rest of the trip, and I could tell she was upset. Why wouldn't she be? Her husband was obviously going nuts.

November 1983: I didn't feel great about taking the anxiety med. It made me feel like I'd given in, been defeated by some weakness of character, but I just couldn't go through the attacks anymore. I'd had it, and if I needed to resort to chemicals to regain my sanity, so be it. When I felt an attack coming on after that, I'd pop a pill. I felt better but suspected it was probably the result of what's called a "placebo effect," more than anything.

Summer 1992: It's been almost ten years since my last Panic Bomb. I'm confident that I'm finally past all that. Maybe the meds have done their job, but I think it probably has more to do with getting older and wiser and cultivating a positive attitude. I'm taking myself off the tranks. No telling what they may do to you over the long haul. I know there are side effect—always are. Damned if I want to find out I got some kind of cancer or brain disorder when I hit sixty. I've read that long-term use of prescription drugs can do something to the body, sometimes really nasty things. So why tempt fate now that I feel all that crap is history? Yes, *I am the master of my soul and the captain of my fate.* Damn right . . . *finally.*

February 1993: These muscle spasms and dizziness must be from overwork. Guess I need to cut back on my hours and get more rest. I'm fine otherwise. Maybe sweating a little more than usual because of having too many layers on in the car. It's really stuffy in here. Hey, man, loosen your collar. What the hell is that creepy noise? It sounds like the Raptors in *Jurassic Park*. Whoa, I feel like I'm free falling . . . plunging down a dark well I won't be able to climb out of. Jesus, the noise is getting louder! What the . . .? There's no air in this goddamn car! Open the frigging window! *I think I'm . . .*

The Humane Thing

This animal is very bad; when attacked it defends itself.
— Anonymous

Old Doc figured it could be the end for Sweet Breeze when the 6-year-old limped into the stable after the last race. Indeed, the mare herself knew that a racehorse that could no longer run was generally put down.

"She's got a major tear in her extensor tendon, so she'll have to be put out of her misery," said Doc to Meg Pelly, who owned the horse.

"Are you sure, Doc? I mean you said the same about Cameroon Doll and Gypsy Gal, and they turned out to be okay. Their owners wouldn't put them down, and they went on to race again after their leg troubles."

"Well, they were the rare exceptions, believe me. I've treated hundreds of horses, and nearly all of the ones that I didn't put down were no good for anything again. Eventually, I was asked to put them down after the horses had suffered longer than they needed to."

Sweet Breeze listened to the conversation, hoping desperately that her owner would choose to spare her. She knew, as did the other horses in the Millbrook Race Track stables, that Old Doc was too quick with the needle and had taken the lives of many animals that were nowhere near ready to go and had no need to be euthanized.

"It's the humane thing to do for these poor injured beasts. They can't speak for themselves, so I'm their voice and, well, . . . you could say their guardian angel."

Angel of death, that's what you are, Doc, thought Sweet Breeze, as she was led into her stall. *Please, Meg, don't let him end my life. I have many good races left in me.*

"Won't even cost you anything to get rid of the carcass . . . er, body, Mrs. Pelly. I have someone who'll take care of that."

Besides, I can use the $200 bucks I'll get, thought Doc, looking through his case for the necessary items to dispatch Sweet Breeze.

"So you really think it's the thing to do? I mean she looks pretty good. The limp isn't that bad," asked Meg, hopefully.

"Believe me, Mrs. Pelly, it's something that will never heal, and to get her to the point that she can even be used to ride kids will cost tons. She'll never be the same again. That's the bottom line, and you can bet her instincts are telling her the same thing. These creatures know these things. "

Sweet Breeze was not having any of what Old Doc was saying. *My instincts? Hooey. What do you know about my instincts? All you care about is selling me to the butchers. Meg, please don't listen to him!! He's a killer. He's taken the lives of too many of my friends just to line his own pockets.*

"Well, if you think it's absolutely necessary, Doc. But I can't watch. I have to leave."

NO! Don't! Please, don't! I only have a minor sprain that will heal quickly.

"It's the best decision, Mrs. Pelly. The horse is in great pain, and she's just not going to be any good to you any more."

That's not true! My leg is only a little sore. In fact, it feels better already. See, I can use it fine, whinnied Sweet Breeze, shifting her weight.

"Whoa, girl. Yeah, see she's hurting. Better let me help her now."

I am NOT hurting, you old windbag. I'll show you. You're not going to peddle me to those meat dealers.

"Goodbye, Sweet Breeze. I'll always remember you," said Meg Pelly, wiping tears away as she left the barn.

Oh no! How could you listen to Old Doc? He's a murderer ... a mass murderer, in fact.

"Okay, girl, let's get this over with. I got other things to do," mumbled the aged veterinarian as he filled a hypodermic with a filmy solution. "You'll be in horsey heaven in no time."

Not if I can help it, thought Sweet Breeze, moving her hindquarter as Old Doc closed in on it with the syringe.

"Don't move. Stay still, you old nag!" growled Doc.

Now ... do it right now! Sweet Breeze told herself.

The 6-year-old kicked her leg with the alleged fatal injury, striking Old Doc in the hand that held the needle. Knocked loose, it landed in his chest and emptied into his heart.

"What did *you*...?" he moaned, clutching at the needle.

Sweet Breeze watched as her would-be assassin fell to the ground unconscious. Within seconds his breathing had stopped.

Sorry I had to lower myself to your behavior, Old Doc, reflected Sweet Breeze, shaking her mane and snorting triumphantly. *It seemed like the humane thing to do.*

The Near Enough

*And she had resolved to live a fool
the rest of her dull life.*
— Francis Beaumont

Susan has a Tootles Baby Doll with beautiful long lashes, and she blinks when you move her. She has a little sailor dress with red stripes. My doll isn't as pretty, but I love her. She has an apron with pockets to put things in. She's not new like Susan's doll, but she's nice enough. I sometimes take her to Susan's house... but not always. Susan lets me play with her doll when I ask.

* * * * *

My house is not as nice as the other houses on our street. They have pretty green lawns and flowers on them. My house has a plastic flamingo in front. My friends make fun of it, but I think they're just jealous because they don't have one at their house. There's an old apple tree in our backyard. It's fun to climb. I guess my house is nice enough. The one across the street has just been painted, and it sparkles when the sun shines on it. I like that.

* * * * *

I wish my hair was curly and blond like Julie Carson's. The boys really like her. She has real smooth skin, no blemishes, and big green eyes. I have two pimples on my right cheek. Julie is very popular. If my eyes were less squinty and my hair wasn't so straight, I bet boys would like me better. I'd be more popular then. My mom says I'm cute, so that's enough, I guess.

* * * * *

Brian Ashby is the school's valedictorian. He's a great student, so smart. A real whiz in math and science. He got accepted at MIT. I graduated third in my class. Could have gone to Boston College. They accepted me, but we don't have the money. State university is fine. A lot of other kids are going there. It's good enough, I think. Everybody congratulated Brian. He was a big deal.

* * * * *

Maybe if I'd gone to a well-known private college I would have gotten a better job, not that my job isn't decent enough. I'm okay with what I do. There's opportunity for advancement. Besides, there are a lot of people who don't even have a job. I hear Susan got an executive position right out of Duke. She's making a lot more money. Good for her.

* * * * *

Sid is fine as a husband. He's not real ambitious, and he could spend more time with our kids, I suppose. Janet is fortunate though. Her spouse, Ben, does it all. He has his own business and manages Little League. All the kids love him. Not hard on the eyes either. That's okay. It's enough that Sid doesn't drink like my parents did. He watches television with the kids on the weekend. They like that a great deal.

* * * * *

Billy and Connie are good kids. I'm blessed, I suppose. I wish they were better students, but they excel in sports, not that Sid cares. Billy can't get up for his paper route, so I deliver his papers most of the time. Connie never seems to come out of her room, but she's just going through what girls her age go through. She really doesn't mean what she says. We're all together, and that's enough. So many families break up. I could never do that.

* * * * *

I'm so happy for Marlene. She just won $10,000 on one of those scratch tickets. Cora got a $1,000 scratcher just last year. Some people are real lucky. Me, too, I guess. I won an Easter basket at a church raffle three years ago. It was lovely. It wasn't any $10,000, but it was enough. We enjoyed it. Sid loved the macadamia nuts. They're very expensive when you buy them separately at the store.

* * * * *

My hubby makes a pretty good salary, but I wish he made enough for us to get a better house, like Susan has. It's incredible. All bright and shiny appliances and granite tops. If we just had a deck and another bedroom, it would make a big difference. At least ours is nearly paid off, and it has good bones, as they say. Maybe I should go back to work, but I feel so out of it. It's been so long. The extra money would help though.

* * * * *

Fifteen fewer pounds would make a noticeable change, I think. Of course, not everyone can look like Susan or Marlene. They both go to the gym and have trainers there. Marlene only has one kid and Susan doesn't have any. That makes a heck of a difference. Having two kids does something to your body. At least it did to mine. I look okay though. I hold my own in the looks department. It's enough. Still, a few pounds off the hips wouldn't hurt. Losing weight is so hard.

* * * * *

Retiring to Florida would be really nice. Everyone seems to be down there now. Almost no friends left up here. But Sid's arthritis isn't that bad, and the house is well insulated against the cold. Have to admit that the ice is scary though. Almost fell down the other day. The twisting made my hip hurt more. I don't want a replacement, but I suppose it's inevitable. We feel fine otherwise, and we'll be able to survive all right as we get older. It's enough . . . really. Not everybody gets to retire to Florida.

* * * * *

Well, Sid's gone . . . died last year. The kids have their own lives, and their children are grown up. I worry about them, but what can I do? Guess I'm near the end of my days on this earth. I can feel it. It's a creeping sort of thing that starts to move faster all of a sudden. I think about my life now and wonder if it's been a good one. As they say, 'A life well-lived.' Have I been happy? Have I been fulfilled? Has it been *enough*? Nearly . . . I *guess*.

The Long and the Short of It

There's nothing in collections of short stories.
— F. Scott Fitzgerald.

"Why are you so gloomy, Hal? You just published another short story collection. What's that, number six?" asked his sister, Jean.

"I'm not gloomy. Just know it won't go anywhere, like the others. The tiny presses have no advertising budgets, so it will sell a few dozen copies . . . mostly to friends."

"Your stuff is so great. Why don't you send it to a big publisher?"

"They don't want story collections, especially if they're not written by big names, and even then they're not enthusiastic about it. I read an article by Stephen King a while back. He said that after he published a best seller, his editor didn't want his book of stories. So how is someone like me ever going to get one of the major houses to publish his stuff? To make matters worse, if you write what they call 'genre' or 'speculative' stories—the stuff I write—publishers *really* don't want it."

"Well, you should try. Don't give up. You really write some incredible stories."

"Thanks, little sister, I appreciate your encouragement. You've been a solid for a long time."

"Hey, what is family for if not to support its talented relatives?"

"Actually, I did send my manuscript to a pretty good press. Not a huge one, but bigger than the places that have published my books in the past."

"Good!"

"I doubt I'll hear from them either, so I'll have to track down another micro-publisher to get my new collection into print."

"What about your novel? Aren't you finished with it? Maybe you could do better with that."

"I'm working on the last chapter. Maybe done in a month. I think it's good."

"Bet it is. You should send it out to a well known publisher, like Random House or Knopf."

"Nah, if you don't have an agent, they won't look at it. Dump it in a slush pile, even if they say they accept unsolicited manuscripts. I'll probably have to go back to one of my itsy-bitsy presses, if I want to get it published"

"Don't do that. Get an agent."

"Wish I could, but it's as hard to get an agent as a good publisher. I've tried . . . believe me. They don't like story collections either."

"So maybe they'll be more receptive to your novel."

"I doubt it."

"Well, don't give up. I'm counting on your fame."

"That could be a bad wager, sis."

"Never a bad wager when it comes to my gifted brother."

"Okay, for that you'll get a free signed copy if it publishes."

"I'm overwhelmed. Look, I better get going. Have to pick up the kid. Besides, I'm beginning to get depressed talking to you. Just believe in yourself like I do."

Jean kissed her brother goodbye and left his apartment. From his window that overlooked the parking lot, Hal watched as she drove away. After a moment he went to his desk and stared at his computer's sleeping screen.

* * * * *

Three weeks after he sent his newest story collection to Words Now Press—a small but more prominent publisher than he'd ever dealt with—he received an email informing him that they were not interested in his submission. However, the editor did urge him to send future work, especially long form prose, saying that she was impressed with the caliber of his writing but rarely contracted story collections. Like other better-established presses, WNP expressed the view that speculative collections generally sold poorly, unless extraordinary.

Well, hell, maybe they'll like my novel, thought, Hal, who had just completed the first lengthy piece of non-speculative fiction in his life. *They invited me to send something else, so I will. Who knows? Worth a shot. No other options anyway.*

He did not have to wait long to hear back from the editor.

We are very much impressed with Web of Dark and are pleased to offer you a contract.

Hal's heart jumped and he let out a yelp of joy. After rereading the email several times to make certain it was real, he called his sister with the news.

"I told you. You're freakin' Hemingway and Faulkner rolled into one. I'm so happy for you, Hal! Now will you let me read your manuscript?"

"No, I'm superstitious about letting anyone see it before it's published . . . even you, dear sister. But I'll let you read the synopsis."

"Jeez, thanks. I'm touched, big brother."

Hal spread the news of the sale of his magnum opus to his parents and as many of his friends as he could reach.

"A *nove*l, Jake. Not a *story collection*, man!" he excitedly told his longtime friend and fellow writer, who had published two small editions of poetry with an eBook press.

Like Hal, Jake had dreamed of one day publishing with a large traditional publisher. He'd envied Hal for his moderate success in getting his works into paperback. Jake believed as Hal did that a book wasn't really a book unless it appeared in tactile form ... not *virtual*. He had actually considered paying to see his poetry between covers, but Hal had dissuaded him by sharing his view that if an author has to pay to see his book in print, then it isn't worth much.

"If you write something of genuine merit, it will get published eventually. Anybody can be published if they pay for it. That's not a *real* book. I'd never do that. I'd be too embarrassed. If I couldn't get my writing published without paying for it, I'd just quit. Self-published books aren't respected. They aren't even reviewed."

"Well, I've heard of some real good writers going that route, but I guess I'd feel a whole lot better if my poetry collection was published with someone else's dime. You think Words Now Press would be interested in my new work? Could you put in a good word for me?"

"Sure, but after they publish my novel. I'm so finished with story collections ... a waste of time. It's novels from here on in ... or *nothing*."

"But your stories are great, Hal. Don't stop writing them. You're brilliant at it."

"You're the only one I know that reads them, Jake, except for my family."

"Well, that's pretty good. My family doesn't download anything. Hardly use computers, so not much of a chance of them seeing them."

"Don't lose hope. You'll get your manuscripts into hard copy."

"Yeah, if I go to Kinkos."

* * * * *

Two weeks after WNP accepted Hal's novel, the contract arrived as an email attachment. He was ecstatic until he reached the last part of the email, which read:

It is a pleasure to be the publisher of your wonderful story collection. The relationship between what you call Chapters has a unity seldom found in story anthologies, but it is clear your work is most appropriate as a collection. We are somewhat unclear by the titling of your stories as Chapters and feel the individual pieces would work better with specific titles. Again, we look forward to producing the eBook of your fine work.

"Collection!? eBook!?" blurted Hal in confusion and dismay.

He sat in stunned silence for several minutes contemplating the exasperating turn of events and then went to his computer and tapped out a response:

Dear Words Now Press,

Here's a NOVEL idea: Go (fill in the blank) yourself!

- Hal Stanley

He hit the reply button and then deleted the publisher's email. Next he went to the kitchen to zap the remains of his coffee cup. As it rotated in the microwave, an idea struck him.

"Damn!" growled Hal returning to the computer. He pressed the Word icon, sighed deeply, and began a new story.

The Window on His World

Absence diminishes commonplace passions,
As the wind extinguishes candles and kindles fire.
— Rochefoucauld

The Wellington was the latest in a wave of high-rise residences constructed on the city's upscale North Side, and all of its units had sold by the time of its delayed completion. It had been pushed a few weeks behind schedule due to an electrician's strike but had finally opened with great fanfare. New occupant Brad Hadley had avoided the cocktail party marking the launch of the 37-story structure, preferring to quietly move into his penthouse condo a day after the gala event. He had considered places in several other new buildings but he had settled on The Wellington because of the stunning view it offered him, especially from the room he would use as his office. Indeed, he'd spend most of his time there while not in his corporate office downtown.

Brad hoped the move would signal a change in his life. For the last decade he had lived in a cluttered one-bedroom apartment near his downtown office. It didn't matter that the rent was far less than he could afford, because he had spent nearly all of his time elsewhere, devoted to his career as a stockbroker. To succeed as he had, Brad had become something of a hermit, forsaking the companionship of his contemporaries. He also had also lost touch with his parents, who had moved to Arizona. His had not been a close family, so their absence from his life was no hardship. Once a practicing Catholic, he had also drifted away from the church. The sole focus of his existence had become the acquisition of wealth. Money was his surrogate God, and at 34 he now had more of it than he ever dreamed possible.

Yet, despite his achievement, he felt a growing void in his life. It was not that he craved anything in particular. He had done fine without close relationships and was very fulfilled in his professional life, yet he experienced a mounting sense of absence. It felt as if there was a hole in his world. *A new environment might help*, he thought, as he committed to buying the $1.7 million condo. His cash payment did not dent what he'd amassed as the result of his hard work and recent major windfalls. He further rewarded himself with a Maserati *GranTurismo*. While he derived a measure of satisfaction acquiring expensive material objects, the novelty of possession quickly faded, and that sense of something lacking in his life took hold again.

* * * * *

Brad now spent most of his workdays in his new residence, only appearing at his company's main office a few times a week to address matters that required his physical presence. While his new surroundings buoyed his mood, they failed to take it to the level he'd hoped such a posh setting would. The most favorable impact on his frame of mind came from the spectacular view from his office window. From it he could take in most of the city's considerable skyline. He had always been attracted to architecture, and the eclectic mix of old and new structures captivated him. He would stare out the window for hours, neglecting his work. At his lowest point, Brad wondered how it might feel to leap from his castle in the sky.

"Better get some window coverings, or I'll be back to sweeping the floor of the Exchange," he mumbled, turning back to his desk.

Yet, after only a few minutes, he was back gazing out of his 37th floor window. This time he noticed there was something slightly askew about the line of buildings that ran the length of the horizon on the other side of the park. Two of the tallest skyscrapers now appeared dwarfed by the lesser structures that had stood next to them. Brad rubbed his eyes and moved closer to the window for a better look. *That can't be*, he thought, straining his eyes to confirm what he was seeing. *They were the tallest,* he mused, while continuing to stare out at the city. *Okay, maybe I wasn't paying enough attention, but I could swear they were . . . .*

Brad returned to his desk and peered at the large monitor's flickering numbers and pulsating lines. For the next couple of hours he tapped at the computer's keyboard nonstop. Finally, he stood and stretched luxuriously. It was twilight, and he turned his attention to the now vibrantly illuminated buildings filling the landscape beyond his window. *Beautiful. Like a fantasyland*, he mulled, in the glow projected by his computer. He sat back down and continued to enjoy the striking view. *It's like another world out there . . . unreal.* It was then that he realized the buildings he had believed were the tallest had been restored to their previous height. *Must have been seeing things this afternoon*, he told himself, only half-assured by his words.

* * * * *

The next day Brad was convinced his eyes were playing tricks on him when those buildings across the green had now changed location, elevation, color, and design. "What's going on with me?" he muttered in growing panic, while scrolling for the number of his eye doctor on his cellphone. He was given an emergency appointment and told not to drive to the ophthalmologist's office. An hour later, Brad jumped into a cab summoned by The Wellington's doorman and arrived at the doctor's office ten minutes before his appointment.

"So you say your sight is distorting? That things don't look right . . . changed?" inquired the eye doctor.

"I know it sounds really weird, but when I look from the window of my condo at the buildings across the park, they keep morphing. Their heights change, and this morning everything about them was different . . . all mixed up."

"How so?"

"Well, their designs seemed changed and they weren't even in the same place. It was like they'd been moved around."

"Is it just the buildings, or do other things change?"

"No, I don't think so . . . no, just the buildings on the North Side. This has never happened to me before, doc."

"I was going to ask you that. Your annual eye exams have been fine, but let's do some checking," said the doctor, dimming the lights and shining a bright beam into his eye. "Looks fine in there. Nothing out of the normal, but we'll do a scan, okay? Just take a few minutes."

While Brad waited for the results, he feared that he might have something wrong with his brain, *maybe a tumor*. His eye doctor's findings deepened his suspicion that something dire might be causing his bizarre visions.

"You're clean. There's nothing wrong with your eyes. Check out perfectly, Mr. Hadley."

"But I'm seeing bizarre things, doc. Maybe I should see a neurologist."

"Why don't you give it a couple days? Stay off the computer and avoid bright lights. It may be a little eye fatigue. You do look a bit tired. Overworking as usual, right?"

Brad agreed to do as the doctor suggested, but he left his office with a sense that he had a problem that a little rest would not address. Then an idea raised his spirits. *Maybe the glass in the window is warped like it is in a funhouse. Could be defective. It's possible.*

As soon as he returned to The Wellington, he conferred with the building's superintendent, who agreed to check it out. And hour later he concluded that the glass in Brad's office window was fine.

"I'd like it changed anyway," responded Brad.

"That will be very costly, Mr. Hadley."

"I understand that. Please have the glass replaced."

While Brad waited for the work to be done, the permutations continued in the fashion they had been occurring. He finally resorted to taping a bed sheet over the window to decrease the anxiety that the ever-changing view was causing him. Finally, a new window was installed, and for several hours the scene beyond the window remained fixed. *Okay, maybe problem solved*, thought Brad hopefully

But it was not to be. When Brad entered his office the next morning, he despaired at the sight that greeted him: A huge gap appeared in the skyline. In the middle of the opening was the spire of a church he had not noticed before. "This is not happening," he groaned, and then dressed and crossed the park to confront the sight tormenting him.

* * * * *

There was no evidence of the buildings Brad had seen so many times from his condo. In their stead were empty lots that reached as far as he could see. There was nothing attesting to their previous existence—no construction equipment or excavations. The ground appeared undisturbed. People streamed up and down the sidewalk without acknowledging the absence of the structures that had been there the previous day. When Brad attempted to ask someone about the bizarre transformation, he was ignored as if he, too, no longer existed.

He took measure of the imposing edifice of the church before him and slowly climbed its steep steps. *St. Agnes? Never heard of it*, thought Brad, reading the gold letters on the large entrance door as he pushed against it. Cool air and the scent of burning candles rushed passed him as he entered the dark interior. As he moved toward the altar, a voice startled him.

"You come to worship, my son?" asked an elderly priest, clutching a rosary.

"No Father . . . no. I don't . . . . I mean I used to but now . . .."

"Now you don't believe? So what brings you here then?"

"What happened to the buildings? They're gone. How can that be?"

"You believe the buildings are gone?"

"Yes, of course, they're gone."

"And that's what brought you here?"

"Yes."

"Well, God acts in strange ways, doesn't he?"

"I don't understand what you're saying."

"You will, my son. You will," replied the priest, who then vanished through an opening on the side of the altar.

"C'mon!" blurted Brad in frustration, "Give me a rational answer, Father. Buildings don't just disappear."

He received no reply from the cleric and after a few moments left the church, heading through the park back toward his condo. Halfway there, he looked back and was stunned to see that the vanished buildings had returned. Where the church had stood was the tallest of the structures extending upward through the clouds. While he stared in disbelief, the old priest's words echoed through his head—*God acts in strange ways.*

The hollowness that had been plaguing him began to diminish during the remainder of his walk home. He finally thought he understood what had happened.

Very strange ways, indeed, he reflected, as a smile transformed his expression.

Eyes of the Beholders

All love at first, like generous wine,
Ferments and frets until 'tis fine;
But when 'tis settled on the lee,
And from th' impurer matter free,
Becomes the richer still the older,
And proves the pleasanter the colder.
— Samuel Butler

Why are my daughters not beautiful, lamented ancient Ireland's King Lugid. T*heir mother is not homely, nor I, but they have the look of Highland banshees. Lugid's witches, I know the peasants say. Why are they cursed with ugliness? Why am I damned to have un*sightly children? No man would want any one of them *as a wife. That is, no man immune to the magic moniker, and what man is? None . . . none in my kingdom, and I thank the Gods for that, for I love my daughters with all of my heart.*

The King's eldest daughter, Feithid, was the first to be married. Next to reach the altar was Mathium. The King's youngest daughter, Bho, was the last to be wed. In each case, Lugid had to invoke the hidden sacred word to make the less than blessed events a reality. Its power rest in its ability to blind suitors to the actual appearance of their brides-to-be.

All that was needed was for the King to utter the magic term into his potential son-in-law's ear and then call for his daughter to appear. What the suitor saw was an idealization of female beauty. But once the suitor was married to the King's daughter, he would slowly see his new wife as she actually was. This resulted in unhappy husbands, all of whom were obliged to remain with the King's daughters or suffer the consequence—beheading.

Finally, the aggrieved husbands decided to murder their unsightly spouses and constructed a plan that would make it appear that they had perished in a tragic accident. This, they believed, would spare them losing their heads and avoid years of living with wives whose appearance they could not bear.

"We will take them to sea, and when we are beyond the sight of the King, heave his loathsome daughters overboard and scuttle the ship. As strong swimmers, we will come to shore and tell Lugid of the terrible tragedy, feigning sorrow over our great loss," suggested the husband of Mathium.

"Yes, and we will be free of our wives' hoary grins and hairy chins," added the spouse of Feithid.

* * * * *

There was a gala celebration when the three would-be widowers gathered their wives for the fateful trip. The King himself saw them off, waving heartily as the three couples climbed the plank to the waiting ship.

"We bid you safe voyage and will await your return with longing hearts," pronounced the King.

There will be little joy in your heart but great joy in ours when we return without your offspring, thought the husbands.

Once the vessel was beyond view of the shore, the King's sons-in-law prepared to set their devious plan in motion.

"Ladies, please join us up on deck," called Mathium's husband.

When the King's daughters joined their husbands, the three men grabbed them, readying to toss them into the churning sea.

"Wait!" shouted one of the King's armored knights emerging from the ship's hold. Two equally stout men with large gleaming swords accompanied him. "Hands off the princesses. You are under arrest for plotting the deaths of the King's daughters."

The King's men seized the stunned husbands and placed them in shackles.

"We were not intending to do our wives any harm, good sirs," protested Feithid's mate.

"Never would we harm our dearest brides," proclaimed Bho's distraught partner.

"What is happening to our husbands?" wailed the King's daughters.

"My Ladies, your husbands were intending to see you drown in order to be rid of you. Your father knew of their plan and put us below to prevent it."

"Surely that cannot be so! My husband loves me," said Mathium, whose words were matched by her hysterical siblings.

The King's guardsmen returned the boat to shore where it was met by the monarch and several other soldiers. His wailing daughters were quickly ushered away as their aspiring assassins were knelt before their liege.

"A blade awaited your necks, my deceitful son-in-laws. That was my intent, but now I see how much my daughters love you, so I will seal you to the fate you abhorred. You are to remain with my daughters for the rest of your lives. You will be closely observed by my soldiers at all times, and should you again conspire to do ill to my beloved children, you will come to your ends."

* * * * *

It was with mixed feelings that the husbands accepted their punishment. But as the years passed, something unexpected happened. Each began to see his respective spouse as she had briefly appeared when the King had invoked the secret word. The sustained beauty they now experienced had grown from the true love their wives felt for them.

While the King could see that the affection of his sons-in-law for his daughters had grown, he required that the executioner's blade always be kept sharp and the secret word near at hand should his daughters need replacement partners.

"Come, dearest husbands," beckoned the princesses, smiling at one another with joyful complicity. "Let us again attempt to voyage the sea."

Burning Desires

At once the wild alarum clashed from all his reeling spires,
And broader still became the blaze, and louder still the din.
— Lord Macaulay

First there's a gentle plume of smoke and then a quiet flicker of light. If all goes right, in a matter of seconds there are flames running across the floor and spilling out of the window. *Magic, it's so magic*, thought Brennan, trembling with delight. He watched at a safe distance as the house he ignited was consumed by fire. It was the fourth time he had torched a structure, and each one had been totally destroyed.

The conflagration and subsequent attempt by firefighters to douse the blaze was both exhilarating and satisfying to Brennan. It was a sensation unlike any other he'd experienced in his 14 years of life. He wasn't sure why, but he always experienced a tremendous sense of release when the objects he targeted were devoured and reduced to rubble. And his impulse to set fires was assuaged for a span of time. But he noticed that the peaceful interlude was diminishing and his need to set another fire was reasserting itself more rapidly.

Brennan knew the term used to describe people like him. *I'm a pyromaniac*, he thought, with a degree of self-recrimination as well as satisfaction. *I'm a dangerous person. I can take away things from people. Things they don't deserve. Maybe I'll burn down Billy's house when no one's there. One more punch from him, and I'm doing it. He better watch out or everything he has will be turned into cinders. That'll teach him to pick on people at school.*

Brennan particularly liked to set fires when it was dark. The bright glow they created against the nighttime sky intensified the thrill he derived from them. It also made it easier to go unseen as he observed the results of his handiwork. He tried to remain close to the scene until the firefighters began to pack up their hoses and axes. But this brought him home late, raising the ire of his mother.

"Do you realize what time it is, mister? Where have you been? This has got to stop. You're just a kid. You're not supposed to be wandering in at any hour. If your father was here . . ."

"But he's not! He ran out on us a year ago, Mom."

"I was just saying . . . Look, let's drop it. Do you want something to eat?"

"No, I'm not hungry. I'm just going to bed."

"Okay, but no more being out this late, Brennan. Promise?"

"Okay . . . promise."

* * * * *

But the following week he returned home late again after watching another of his carefully planned immolations bring down a building. This time he knew his mother would not be home until near midnight because of a date with her new boyfriend. While he was upset that she was seeing someone other than his father, he was pleased that it gave him an opportunity to be out later than usual without incurring her wrath. The more she dated, the more he started fires.

Brennan had one rule about incinerating places. He would avoid taking a life at all costs. This required that he observe the comings and goings of people living in or working at his targeted sites. It was time-consuming but necessary. The thought of killing someone horrified him.

News of his devastating acts filled the local newspapers and broadcast outlets. *Be careful. You could get caught. They're looking for an arsonist. Better keep to residential buildings. The police are watching businesses and offices*, Brennan advised himself. *Maybe I should stop doing this. Sooner or later someone will see me.*

For a while, Brennan was able to suppress his urge to set fires, but it finally became too much for him. *I need to do this. I really, really need to do this.* And he did. In the course of two weeks, he had burnt down three more houses. His appetite for producing infernos continued unabated and, in fact, was on the rise.

* * * * *

On the day he had planned to set his next blaze, he was awakened by a knock on his bedroom door.

"Brennan, can I come in?"

"What, Mom? It's Saturday. Let me sleep."

"I need to talk to you."

Before he could protest further, his mother entered. Her face was pale and glistened with tears.

"What's the matter, Mom?"

"I have something very painful to tell you."

"Huh . . . what?"

His mother hesitated and after a deep, tortured breath said what was on her mind.

"Daddy has died, honey."

"No! How?" Brennan gasped.

"In a fire. The house he was renting caught fire. I didn't even know he was still living in town. And not even that far from us."

"A fire. He died in a fire? Where?"

"Over on Mill Court. It's only a couple of miles from here, I'm so sorry, honey. This is just so terrible."

Brennan turned away from his mother. Almost instantly he knew he had set the fire that took his father's life.

"I don't know what's going to happen next. I guess it's up to his family to make funeral arrangements."

"Are you sure it was him? Maybe they made a mistake. I was sure no one . . . Why would he be living so close to us? He disappeared. We never heard from him."

"They made a positive ID. It was him, Brennan. I'm not sure why he was back, or if he ever really left. Maybe he wanted to be close to us . . . or *you*."

* * * * *

For several months, Brennan felt adrift, confused, and heartsick. His compulsion to set fires had been supplanted by his sense of guilt over the death of his father. He remained in his room contemplating his horrific deed and only emerged when necessary. All he could think about was that fact the he was his father's murderer. His mood sank further when his mother informed him of her plans to marry again. He'd only met her boyfriend on a couple of occasions and had taken an immediate dislike to him.

"Why are you doing this?" he screamed at his mother.

"Because I love him, and you'll learn to like him, Brennan. Just give him a chance."

"I hate adults! You're all the same. Only care for yourselves. Get out of my room!"

In the days that followed, Brennan could feel the powerful urge to set fires reassert itself. He fought it as hard as he could, but it became too powerful for him to keep at bay.

"I can't do it again! I shouldn't do it again! I really, really need to do it again!" he screamed into his pillow.

As the sun disappeared over the horizon, Brennan gathered his matches and accelerant and left the house.

Tuna Melts

All theory, dear friend, is grey, but the golden [sea] of actual life springs ever green.
— Goethe

"New Orleans reminds me of dark death, Hank."

"How so, Fred? Explain what you're saying, my friend."

"This is a city where they stack corpses on top of one another ten high to make room for new arrivals."

"A sensible use of limited urban space, I would say. So what's your point?"

"All those decaying bodies dissolve into a common stew that eventually seeps into Lake Ponchartrain.

"Okay, I think I'm with you so far."

"This waste coils out to the Gulf and is consumed by the Albacore."

"Nice to know that human remains benefit nature."

"Yeah, but Fishermen return the decedent cells to the dinner tables of the homes and restaurants throughout this area."

"Sounds anthropomorphic, Fred. A little like reincarnation."

"Hank, I think I've solved the age-old question of what causes multiple personality disorder . . . *seafood*."

Nailed

Money speaks sense in a language all people understand.
— Aphra Behn

Lotus Nails was an ever-expanding enterprise with at least a dozen chairs and as many manicurists. Billie Seymour recalled when it was half the size, and how much she had liked the intimacy of it back then. *They surely are industrious people*, she thought, taking her accustomed seat near the front of the parlor.

"Hello Miss Seymour. You look very nice today. I like your outfit. It pretty," greeted Sovann Lim, a diminutive, middle-aged Cambodian man, with a formidable mole on his upper left cheek.

It was exactly how he had greeted Billie every time over the four years she'd been his regular customer. His English was barely intelligible, so conducting a conversation with him was very difficult. Billie tried the first few times he did her nails, and then she all but gave up. It just took too much of her energy to try.

He's been in this country for years and still can't speak decent English, mulled Billie, reaching for a magazine in the hope he would not attempt to engage her in further feeble conversation. That was her regular strategy, and it had worked well enough.

During recent visits, she had become convinced that Sovann and his fellow manicurists were talking about her, indeed possibly making fun of her. From the corner of her magazine, she would spy them looking her way while they chattered in their cacophonous tones. A chorus of shrill laughter would suddenly erupt, and they would quickly turn away from her as she lowered her magazine. *What do they find so amusing about me?* she wondered. *I know I'm a large woman. Anyone would appear huge next to their scrawny bodies. But what is so amusing to make them laugh like that? Maybe it's not me. Could be something else, of course. But I don't think so . . .*

* * * * *

Billie's suspicions finally got the better of her, and she decided to take action. The next time she visited Lotus Nails, she recorded their conversations on her smart phone while having both her finger-and toenails trimmed and polished. She had decided to take it to an Asian language professor at the local college and pay him to interpret it.

"Yes, I do understand Cambodian, but I usually don't translate private conversations," said Professor Kim.

"It's really not private. They knew I was recording them. I'm just fascinated with the sounds of the language and want to start understanding it. I wish State U. offered Cambodian. I'd love to take a course in it."

"Well, I wish they would, too. I've been trying to convince the administration to offer an introductory course in Cambodian, because there's a sizeable population of them in our community. They own many local businesses, so it would make sense to offer it. Perhaps you could write a request to the dean?"

"Of course, I'd be happy to. I'd be the first to enroll."

"So what is it you want me to listen to?"

The professor wrote out a translation on a lined pad as Billie played her recording for him.

"Nothing very exciting, I'm afraid. Although they certainly are enthusiastic."

"What are they talking about, professor?"

"Business and investment plans. Apparently they're pooling their resources to purchase property. Leave it to immigrants to act like true American capitalists. These folks are very ambitious."

"That's all? Nothing else. Why are they laughing so much?"

"Excited by their ideas, I guess. Oh, one of the women did make reference to you."

"Ah ha. What did she say?"

"Something about liking your outfit."

"That's it?"

"Afraid so."

* * * * *

Billie left the professor feeling dissatisfied with the outcome. *The Cambodians were so animated. Too animated to be talking about such dull topics as real estate. And why did they laugh when I looked at them? And what about professor Kim, huh? Another inscrutable Oriental. And he probably knows them. It's a cabal against this country's real citizens.*

Still troubled, Billie decided not to return to Lotus Nails and soon located a parlor operated by non-Asians. On her fourth visit there, a newspaper article caught her attention.

A local business group has announced plans to build a shopping mall in the vicinity of East Avenue and Torrance Boulevard. They indicate that two major national retailers will anchor the proposed center.

Oh, that will be great, thought Billie. *We need something like that, and it will be so convenient to where I live. I wonder where it will be exactly?*

A letter she received a month later told her just where the new mall would be located. Even her neighbors could hear her screams.

"My apartment complex is being torn down to make room for the mall!" she blurted, reading further. "The land was purchased by . . .!" at this point, Billie slumped into a chair. "by the *Lotus* Corporation?"

Billie tossed the eviction notice to the floor and leapt to her feet again, her fists waving wildly in the air.

"I knew they were talking about me!" she bellowed at the top of her lungs. "I just *knew* it!"

Somewhere Out There

> *It should be noted that children at play are not playing about; their games should be seen as their most serious-minded activity.*
> — Montaigne

Little Brodie stood on the rise behind his family's house and stared at the vast expanse of high plains that stretched to the horizon in every direction. He knew that the town of Seymore was somewhere out there and that his daddy had gone there a month ago and never returned. His mother had driven them out to the western Nebraska town several times and had inquired about her husband, but nobody had seen him.

"How could he do this . . . just disappear on us?" Jenny Parker had repeated in a tone her son had never heard before as they rode back home.

Little Brodie tried to wrap his young mind around the idea that his father might have literally disappeared. *How did someone do that?* wondered the seven-year-old. *Was he there and then suddenly not? Poof, just like that gone? Daddy must have had magic, like on TV.*

People had done just that on some of the programs he had seen, and the notion that his father might have possessed the ability to vanish fascinated him. But it also scared him a little, too. *Maybe daddy was right there with them now, but they could not see* him. *Why would he not let them see him? C'mon, Daddy, let me see you*, he would mutter longingly as he lay in bed unable to sleep because of the pain he felt over his father's absence. *Please, daddy, let me see you. I won't tell anyone . . . promise.*

His pleas went unanswered, as did his mother's.

"How come the police are looking for Daddy? Did he do something wrong?" asked Brodie.

"Of course not, honey. They're just trying to help us find Daddy and bring him home to us."

Jenny tried as best she could to explain to Brodie that his dad had suffered from post-traumatic stress disorder since returning from service in Afghanistan.

"Daddy sometimes feels bad about being away at the war. It made him unhappy, and he's been trying to forget about it. But it takes time to get better."

"You can disappear when you're sad? Did that make him disappear, mom?"

"I think it might have. Don't worry. I think he'll come back soon . . . when he is happy again."

* * * * *

Another month went by with no sightings of Kyle Parker by Jenny or the authorities. However, this was not the case for Little Brodie, who had seen his father four times during his wanderings in the open spaces surrounding his house. When he first reported seeing his father to his mother, Jenny was surprised and excited.

"Where is he, honey? Is he coming home? Did he tell you where he'd been?"

"No, we just played, and then he disappeared again."

"Did he say where he was going, Brodie? Please, tell Mommy everything you remember."

"He said back to the clouds," replied Brodie, his brow scrunched contemplatively. "I guess that's where he disappears to."

"Honey, are you sure you really saw Daddy?"

"We played Frisbee, and then when I threw it really high,

Daddy disappeared again."

"Honey, are you making this up because you want to see Daddy so bad?"

"No, Mommy, he's somewhere out there," answered Brodie, pointing toward the mid-afternoon sun.

"In the clouds?"

"Yes, in the clouds," said Brodie, his big blue eyes looking skyward.

When Brodie told his mother he had seen his father again, she began to become concerned about her son's emotional wellbeing.

"I think you're making it up, sweetie. Your father went away. You know that."

"Yes, he *disappeared*. But he comes back and we have fun," protested Brodie.

"What does he tell you?"

"That he loves us."

"Look, honey. I want you to stay closer to the house. Play in the backyard. I don't want you wandering off to where I can't see you."

"But if I don't go out there, I won't see him, and I want to play with Daddy," said Brodie, pointing toward the empty distance.

"Please, just stay in the yard for now, sweetie."

* * * * *

Growing increasingly anxious about her son's behavior, Jenny contacted Family Services in Seymore and was put in touch with one Mrs. Dalkey, a child psychologist. After a lengthy phone conference with the therapist, a date and time was arranged for her to make a visit to the Powells' house to meet and observe Brodie.

"It would be best to see Brodie in his own environment, so I'll make the trip. I don't mind really. It's a chance to get out of the office," said Dalkey after Jenny expressed concern that she had to travel nearly twenty miles.

"Well, I'll make lunch. Thank you so much. I've been really worried about Brodie."

Two days hence, Mrs. Dalkey arrived at the Parker residence. In the interim, Brodie had reported seeing his father again.

"In the yard? You saw him in our yard?"

"No, he didn't come close. He stayed out there," replied Brodie, flicking his hand toward an area far beyond the wood fence that bordered the property.

When Mrs. Dalkey arrived, the two women sat in the kitchen and discussed the situation further. When it was time for lunch, Jenny called for Brodie, but he did not appear.

"Kids are always somewhere that blocks their mom's voice," joked Mrs. Dalkey, recognizing Jenny's anxiety.

Jenny went outside and walked around the house, but there was no sign of her son. *I told him to stay in the yard. Why . . . why is this happening? Where are you, Kyle? Look what's happened because you disappeared on us*, lamented Jenny, returning inside the house.

"I'm sorry, Mrs. Dalkey. He must have wandered away. He's probably looking for his father.

"No problem, Mrs. Parker. I can return at a better time."

"Please stay for lunch. I've made us salad and chicken sandwiches. Besides, I could use the company."

"Of course, dear. I'd love to. Thank you," said Mrs. Dalkey, patting Jenny's arm.

* * * * *

A mile across a parched field that led to the dirt road that ran to the Parker's house, Little Brodie noticed the dusty contrail of an approaching vehicle. As it got closer he recognized it. "Daddy's truck. He's come to play with me again!" he yelped, joyously.

The battered Ford pickup stopped, and Brodie's father jumped out and ran up to his son with his arms spread wide. He scooped the boy off the ground and held him tightly.

"Daddy, you brought your truck this time!" said Brodie, delighted.

"Huh? *This time . . .?*"

"You didn't bring it before."

"Before . . . ?"

"Yeah, when we played out there, Daddy" said Brodie, pointing across the plains.

"Sure . . . *okay*. Whatever you say, son. So, how's my Little Brodie? I've missed you, boy! I'm so sorry I left you guys. I just had to work out a few things. But I'm back, and I'm better. Let's go see Mommy."

Kyle carried his son to his truck and placed him in the passenger seat.

"You want to drive, kiddo?"

"Yeah, Daddy, let me drive."

"Maybe when you're a little bigger," chuckled Kyle, patting his son's cheek after climbing behind the wheel.

"Mommy cried because you disappeared. How did you make yourself disappear, Daddy?"

"Sometimes you feel you have to disappear. You'll understand when you're older."

"Will I disappear, Daddy?

"I hope you won't have to. Now. Let's get home."

* * * * *

When Jenny heard the sound of the approaching vehicle, she knew it was her husband's pickup.

"Oh, my God. Kyle? It's Kyle!" shouted Jenny, jumping up from the kitchen table and dashing to the front door.

As Kyle drove up to the house, Jenny ran to meet him.

"Honey, I'm sorry . . . so sorry! My head was all messed up, and I didn't want to subject you and Brodie to the demons in there."

"You didn't have to disappear, Kyle. We could have worked things out together. Got help."

The Parkers stood wrapped in a long embrace and then climbed the porch steps, where Mrs. Dalkey stood taking in the scene before her. As they passed her, Little Brodie spoke.

"See, I told you I *saw* Daddy!"

Finding Poetry on Mars

Verse foreign doth now proclaim thy fate.
— Anonymous

The commander of NASA's third manned mission to Mars reported back to Earth on something quite extraordinary. His crew had discovered a foot square piece of igneous rock with what appeared to be some kind of writing on its surface. The "item," as Houston referred to it, was found near the Hottah outcrop, where the *Ares 3* mission had landed.

The discovery had prompted Mission Control to order the crew to leave the Red Planet just three days into its exploratory assignment. When Commander Mulgrave informed his team of the decision there was near mutiny.

"We're supposed to have 26 more days here!" protested Dr. Helen Morris, the mission's astrophysicist. "We're going to scrub all the other research because of this? That's nuts!"

"Helen, this is not an *insignificant* find. I'm sure you're aware of that. What we have here appears to be evidence of life beyond our own planet. Jesus, think about that!"

"Probably something left over or planted by one of the earlier missions."

"You know better, Helen. Those missions were no where near this site."

"Look, please ask Mission Control for a couple more days.

You know I have a crucial experiment to perform. What harm can a couple days cost?"

"No can do. I have strict orders to get us back home. No loopholes in that. I know this makes you very upset ... makes everyone upset, because we all had important work to do here. But orders are orders."

"I simply can't believe this!"

"C'mon, Helen, we're bringing something back of historical importance. Something that may change how humans think of the universe. That's pretty damn remarkable, I'd say. *Ares 3* and her crew will be known for that."

"*But...*" moaned Morris, exasperated.

"We'll launch at 1700 hours."

* * * * *

It would take nearly four months for *Ares 3* and her crew to return to Earth. To the many who were curious about the mission's early return, the official story concerned a malfunction in the space vessel's oxygen renewal system. Members of the thwarted mission were told to say nothing about their unique discovery.

"Not a peep about this. If it is what it looks like, and I'm pretty sure it is, the world is in for one hell of a shock," repeated Commander Mulgrave, as *Ares 3* began to feel the pull of the Earth's atmosphere.

However, his order had gone unheeded by Helen Morris, who had sent her husband a brief message about the mysteriously engraved rock shortly after its discovery. She hadn't reminded him not to say anything because it had never before been necessary to do so. Eric Morris was a person who knew how to keep a secret and always had ... except for on this one occasion when he let slip to a colleague that *Ares 3* had seemingly discovered evidence of intelligent life on Mars.

"Helen told you this? My God, this is the greatest discovery in history. How? I mean *what...?*" asked Cary Hamilton, stunned.

"I shouldn't have said anything. Promise you won't talk about this," pleaded Eric.

"That's just mind-boggling. Holy shit! It's going to turn everything upside down, man," said Cary, shaking his head in awe.

"You heard what I said, Cary?"

"Huh? Sure . . . but what is it? I mean, *what* did they find . . . ? "

* * * * *

By the time *Ares 3* had returned home, word of the discovery had, of course, leaked and then spread like wild fire. Virtually all media buzzed with the news. Throughout the world, newspaper and video news headlines told of the astonishing event.

> **We Are Not Alone! Life Found on Mars . . .**
> **Extraterrestrial Intelligence Exists . . .**
> **Proof of Life Beyond Earth Discovered . . .**
> **A Message From Aliens Being Decrypted . . .**
> **Martians Communicate to Humans . . .**

Religious groups went on the defensive immediately, discounting the find as inconclusive. "It is likely something left or discarded by previous Mars unmanned probes and manned missions," declared the Vatican Information Service.

Meanwhile, the Earth-bound humans waited anxiously for the message to be deciphered. Renowned linguists and archeologists invited by NASA worked to reveal the meaning of the text on the Martian rock. Within a week they had a partial decryption.

"One of the words means 'alien,' in Aramaic," declared Carter Hyde of Harvard.

Two weeks later, they revealed what they believed was a complete phrase:

> *Whether alien or native*

"May be from an early Semitic poem," observed Stanford's Myles Lendon.

The head of NASA, Chuck Peel, immediately contacted the White House, as was consistent with official protocol in matters of grave importance.

"What does it mean?" asked the president."

"We're running a search at the moment, Mr. President. As soon as we know, you'll know, sir. There's some thinking that it may be a fragment of verse. Dr. Hyde feels it might be a biblical excerpt."

Dr. Hyde's hunch was quickly verified as a line from Leviticus 24:16.

"Well, I think the religious community will be happy to hear that," responded the president, when informed about the writing. "Wait on your news conference until I've contacted several key world leaders. I'll let you know when you can announce to the world that NASA may have found proof of the existence of God. Congrats, Chuck!"

He added light heartedly, "This ought to get you that budget increase."

The first person the president called was the Pope, who was understandably delighted by the news. The Vatican immediately issued a press release, which began thusly:

> **Our Lord God, creator of the universe, has issued forth evidence of his presence on a planet beyond our own. Surely, as man continues his space explorations, His words will be found throughout the Cosmos . . .**

The leaders of Communist countries were somewhat less enthusiastic when informed of the text by the US President.

"It would seem premature to make such a claim, especially since there are said to be more words present on the Martian artifact," responded the president of the People's Republic of China.

* * * * *

As work continued to decode the Martian object, churches around the world reported increased attendance. At the same time, the incidents of violence and crime, in general, declined everywhere. In an address viewed worldwide, the Pope proclaimed the date of the Martian discovery to be a new High Holy Day of Obligation, saying:

> **Just as we observe the events of Christ's birth and his Ascendancy to Heaven, we shall now observe the day when He first spoke to us from Mars...**

Six weeks after the president received the call from NASA informing him of the first deciphered phrase carved into the Mars rock, he was told that the rest of the words had finally been determined.

"Great! So what are they? More of the same, I assume. I mean, more Bible-related scripture, right?" asked the president.

"Well, no, sir. We're not sure what the origin is . . . now. It's clearly not religious in nature. That we're pretty sure about," replied the head of NASA, hesitantly.

"Okay, so let's hear what you got, Chuck."

"The full text is laid out like a poem . . . a quatrain. It says, ah . . ."

"Go ahead! Why the hesitation, Chuck?" blurted the president.

The NASA official gathered his breath and spoke softly.

"Sir, it says:

> *Whether alien or native*
> *Let it now be known*
> *Life in this galaxy ends*
> *When this writing is shown*"

After a prolonged pause, the president was about to say something . . .

The Valet

Experience teaches slowly, and at the cost of mistakes.
— J.A. Froude

For lack of a better opportunity after college, Percy Barron had started parking cars for CafE Balthazar on Wednesday. Soon he learned that Friday and Saturday nights were twice as busy.

"You'll have to park at one of the annexes," he was told by the valet supervisor, Mark Gorley. When he was told that there were six of them sprawled across the city, he was taken aback.

"How do I get back to the restaurant from the ones across town?" he had asked, and was told he would have to use public transportation.

"The subway?" he had replied, nonplussed.

"If you're near one. Mostly you got to take the bus. Don't worry. You can usually find a stop at the closer lots. Then you just jog your ass back."

His fellow valets did not instill confidence that he would find a ride close to the remote lots.

"The farther out ones are harder. On weekends the closer lots are usually solid, but once you're here a while, the attendants at those will help you out. Of course, at first, you got to help them out."

"Help them out?" asked Percy.

"Yeah, you know. Grease their palm," said his coworker, rubbing his fingers over his thumb.

"You mean you've got to tip them to get a place?"

"Yeah, and that comes out of *your* gratuities."

"That doesn't sound fair," complained Percy.

"Well, it evens out, because if you have to take city transportation to get back from one of the far-off lots, it will cost you almost as much, especially if you take a cab."

"Still . . ."

By the time Friday night arrived, Percy had somewhat come to terms with the arrangement, although he remained unhappy with it. *Maybe I'll get lucky and there'll be spaces at the nearby lots without having to tip for one*, he thought, climbing into the BMW X6 he had to park away from the restaurant's own lot.

At the first lot, a sign read 'full,' but rather than negotiate for a parking spot, he drove on to the next closest lot. Again, he encountered a sign indicating the absence of available space. *I'll be damned if I'm going to pay to park the restaurant's customer's cars. That's bull*, he thought, heading to the next designated lot. It, too, was full, but this time, Percy decided to see what he could do to get a place for the BMW.

Not going to drive around all night.

"I might have someplace for the Beemer. It depends," said the attendant, with a knowing smirk.

Percy pulled two singles from this pocket and held them out. The attendant snickered and made a face.

"Ten bucks, man."

Without responding, Percy drove off. "Ten dollars! That's nuts! It's going to cost me to work at CafE Balthazar at this rate. No freaking way!" grumbled Percy.

He met the same fate at the next two lots and reluctantly headed to the last lot on the list, which happened to be in a rundown part of the city known for its high crime rates. *I'm going to have to walk miles to catch a bus if I make it through this slum without being jumped*, Percy moaned. To his further chagrin, that last lot—squeezed between two abandoned buildings—also displayed a sign indicating a lack of parking spots.

Percy entered the dilapidated attendant's shack and peered through its dim light for the person on duty.

"Hello . . . anybody here?"

"Yeah, what you want? Lot's full, man," growled a voice from behind the counter.

A disheveled head supported by a squat body slowly emerged.

"Need a space for a vehicle from CafE Balthazar."

"Ain't got none. You didn't see the sign, dude?"

Percy removed a five-dollar bill from his pocket and waved it in front of the unshaven attendant.

"Ten, man. Take it or leave it."

Shit . . . fine. What else can I do? Boy, I'm going to bitch about this when I get back to the restaurant, thought Percy, his anger surging.

"You got change? I only have a twenty," asked Percy.

"Hold on. Let me check," said the attendant, opening a small metal box. Minutes passed as he searched for change.

C'mon, for God's sake. You can't count? What's up with you? Percy wondered.

"Hey, man, I got to get back to the restaurant."

"You want the space or not, dude? I'm looking for the ten bucks you need back, but I only got eight. Here, I'll give you the other two bucks I owe you when you come back again."

Yeah, like that will happen. Damned if I'll ever come back here.

Percy reluctantly took the eight dollars.

"Keys in the ignition," he said, turning to leave.

"Hold on. You need a receipt."

Shit, it'll be sunrise before I get back . . . if I get back at all, thought Percy. "Fine, fine, give me the receipt," he snapped.

"Where the hell's my pen?" grumbled the middle-aged man, rummaging through a stack of papers.

This a-hole is deliberately delaying me! Frigging jerk!

The attendant finally wrote out the receipt and handed it to Percy.

"You want an IOU for the two bucks? I'll give you one if you want it. It's a lot of dough," said the attendant, with a snide grin.

"Where do I get a bus around here?" asked Percy, coldly.

"There's a stop up on Claremont."

"Where's that?"

"About six blocks that way," said the attendant, pointing his finger. "But I ain't sure they run this late."

"That's great!" spit Percy, on his way out of the shack.

As soon as he emerged from it, he stopped in his tracks. "*What the...?*"

The BMW had already been stripped of its tires and was up on blocks. Percy turned back to the shack, but the door was now locked.

"Hey, open up! The car has been vandalized . . . *stripped*. C'mon!"

There was no response, and Percy kicked at the door in a rage. "You son of a bitch. I'm going to call the cops!"

"Get out of here, or I'm going to call the cops on *you*! This is private property!" returned a voice from inside the shack.

Percy stood in the dark contemplating his next move. He then took a photo of the dismantled Beemer with his cellphone and forwarded it to his boss with the following text:

"Finally found a parking space. Come and get the car. You can use public transportation to get here. I *quit*!"

Life's Priorities

The ruling passion, be it what it will,
The ruling passion conquers reason still.
— Alexander Pope

Gus was reading the latest edition of *Sports Illustrated* when he turned his attention to CNN.

The asteroid is now said to be on a collision course with Earth. It was expected to come within 50 thousand miles of the planet, but last night the Crimean Astrophysical Observatory recalculated its path and discovered it is headed directly toward us...

Gus stood up and moved closer to the wall-mounted flat screen. "What the...?"

It is calculated to be a mile wide. Experts say it possesses the equivalent of a 900-kiloton bomb, enough to create massive destruction to the planet and likely end all forms of life...

"Okay! Okay!" he shouted angrily. "What about the *football* scores!!"

Michael C. Keith is the author of more than 20 books on electronic media, among them *Talking Radio, Voices in the Purple Haze, Radio Cultures, Signals in the Air*, and the classic textbook *The Radio Station* (now *Keith's Radio Station*). The recipient of numerous awards in the academic field, he is also the author of dozens of articles and short stories and has served in a variety of editorial positions. In addition, he is the author of an acclaimed memoir—*The Next Better Place* (screenplay co-written with Cetywa Powell), a young adult novel—*Life is Falling Sideways*, and seven other story collections—*Of Night and Light, Everything is Epic, Sad Boy, And Through the Trembling Air, Hoag's Object, The Collector of Tears*, and *If Things Were Made To Last Forever*. He has been nominated for two Pushcart Prizes and a PEN/O.Henry Award and was a finalist for the National Indie Excellence Award for short fiction anthology and a finalist for the 2013 International Book Award in the "Fiction Visionary" category. www.michaelckeith.com